JEWELS

Lakisha Spletzer

Illustrated by JD Hollyfield

ISBN: 1449502075

EAN: 9781449502072

Printed in the United States of America by CreateSpace

Author Acknowledgments

I have to say that without a lot of support and help, none of the stories that swirl around in my head would have ever made it to the light of day. With that being said, I want to thank Lyn Ehley, Allan Baker, and Meredith West for helping me edit and smooth out this novel until it was the gem it could be. I want to thank Amiee Marshall and Earl G. Ehley, Sr., for being such avid readers of the rough drafts. Your encouragement and enthusiasm for the story means a lot.

I definitely want to thank Dianne Dykstra for putting up with my endless prattle and excitement as I wrote this story. Thank you to the Lakes Region librarians Shannon, Mickey, Cheryl and all the others, who put up with my boundless energy and constant showings of this book's artwork.

Illustrator Acknowledgments

Thanks to...

...my parents for the ever present support and guidance.

...my sweet love, Amy, for the compassionate patience and the soothing love.

...my sweet son, don't ever let anyone stop you from your hearts desire.

...Kisha for the constantly engaging conversation and awesome friendship over the years.

...my papaw, you are deeply missed.

JEWELS

Chapter 1

Special Lieutenant Jewels Enbran turned and admired her partner's physique. Colonel Jeremy Lingley was thirty-four, and fifteen years her senior, but that didn't matter to Jewels. All her partners were older. They had to be to work with her and her special "need."

"Relax, Jewels. I'm sure it's nothing major," Jeremy advised from his seat by the window.

Jewels fidgeted with the starched collar of her military uniform. The strict dress code always made her uncomfortable. Her dark brown curly hair was slicked back and held in place by a white hair clip. Her olive skin and violet eyes were complimented by the dark blue blouse and snug pleated skirt.

"If you say so." She shrugged and resisted the urge to pace. Waiting had never been her strong suit nor was standing on ceremony, two things the military had in abundance.

::I see that look in your eyes. If they notice your anxiety, you won't have a leg to stand on. ::

She grimaced. ::I thought we agreed, Jeremy, no telepathy,:: she joked, too nervous to hide her unease. It wasn't like she hadn't been here before, in the North America United Peoples Organization Headquarters, receiving orders. It was, however, the first time she would be meeting with the President. The President ran the UPO and

1

dictated worldwide policy for the planet Earth.

::They don't need to know everything about us. There are surveillance bugs scattered through the room. I can "feel" their metallic buzz. You would think by now that the higher-ups would recognize that particular talent of ours.:: Jeremy stretched casually, his gaze on the Picasso picture hanging on the wall near her.

Jewels tugged at her collar again, calmly reached out and touched the artwork. With her electrokinesis she traced the flow of electricity until she located the bug in the wall.

::Wow, this is the smallest one yet. I bet if an enemy did a scan it wouldn't register.:: With little effort she disabled it just for fun. Might as well give the eggheads something to fret over.

::Told you. Uh, oh. I do believe we are about to have company.:: Jeremy came to his feet as the door across the room opened.

::Ugh, show time.:: She was less than thrilled. Jeremy and she had just finished a job in the Australian Outback. They both had been hoping for some R & R, but on the return trip they were rerouted to the North Continent HQ. No one would tell them anything. Hush-hush operations made her paranoid. She straightened and eyed the doorway. Time to show a united front. Jewels walked over to her partner, her face expressionless as three men poured into the foyer.

::I don't recognize any of them. Jeremy, do you know them?::

::No, I don't. It'll be okay, Jewels. Play it close to the vest until we know the score. I won't put you in danger.::

His fierce protectiveness made her want to grin and she checked that impulse quick. Anything other than stoicism in this place made you a target. She assessed the three officers. Two bore General bars and the third, a lean, weasel-face man, had no identifiable marks.

::Do you think he's Special Ops?::

::Possibly. Or he could be part of the Diplomatic Corps. Who knows? They're coming this way. Whatever you do, behave and be polite,:: Jeremy admonished.

She didn't get a chance to reply. The two generals and their companion were standing before them. She snapped to attention and focused on keeping her breathing even and calm.

The shorter of the two generals addressed them first. He looked to be in his fifties and was beginning to go bald. He, however, did not appear to be overweight. Instead muscles bulged underneath his uniform jacket.

"Lieutenant Enbran. Colonel Lingley. At ease. I am General Hinson. This is General Zenath and Colonel Brion from Intel. If you will come this way, the President is waiting."

"Yes Sir!" Jewels and Jeremy replied in unison before falling in line behind the officers. She was brimming with curiosity, but behaved herself. Answers would be forthcoming.

The room they entered was large and filled with priceless artwork. In the middle sat a large maple desk. It was the man behind the desk that caught Jewels by surprise. She'd never seen footage of the President and had pictured him as being tall with arresting features.

The man before her was anything but arresting. A jagged scar ran across his face starting at the right temple and ending at the bottom of his left cheek. Cold gray eyes raked over her and Jewels felt exposed.

She heard a click and then a whirring noise. Her gaze slid down and she gaped. Jewels was fixated on the President's cybernetic arm. No wonder he didn't do vids! The public would not take kindly to the news that the most important position on the planet was held by a cyborg.

::Jewels, you're gawking. Close your mouth and pay attention!::

A brilliant shade of hot pink stained her cheeks. *::Sorry, Jeremy! I didn't know he was, well you know...::*

::Just stay focused, Kid. We don't want to get on his bad side,:: Jeremy warned.

The mental exchange took mere seconds yet the heat of the President's gaze made Jewels feel like a naughty child with one hand in the sweets jar.

"Are the two of you finished talking?"

Jewels stared, caught herself and stammered, "Sorry, Sir! We didn't mean to be rude!"

The President waved her excuse off. "Don't worry, young lady. I'm not angry. Fascinated, yes. I would never have known you were speaking telepathically if I didn't have the psi-sensors installed." He turned to address the room's other occupants. "Colonel Brion, she is everything you promised and a definite solution to our problem."

"She is the best, Mr. President. This partnership has worked the most efficiently out of all her pairings to date. And with Colonel Lingley's help, Lt. Enbran's number of successful missions is the highest in the history of Psi-Ops."

Jewels squirmed, embarrassed by the praise. *::They want*

4

something. I wish they would just tell us.::

::Patience, Jewels. Let them talk. Remember, even the most innocent of phrases carry double meanings in our world.::

::I know. I know.::

"...They come highly recommended. All they need is the clearance, a time, place and date, and we're in business," Colonel Brion concluded and smiled.

It wasn't a nice smile and Jewels shivered. That man she needed to be careful around. He saw much and possibly plotted even more. After all, he was in Intel.

"Thank you, Colonel Brion, but you didn't have to sell me on their skills. I see it right before my eyes." The President studied Jewels for a long moment before speaking. "Young woman, you and your partner will be taking part in a cultural exchange of sorts."

Jewels was confused. There were no undiscovered cultures left on earth.

"I see you're dying to ask a question. Don't worry, General Zenath shall explain."

The tall dark-skinned General stood, cleared his throat and took over the conversation. "Six months ago, one of our space probes picked up activity in an adjacent unexplored galaxy. Imagine our surprise, when a species, known as the Gatoans, contacted us via our probe. Since then, we have established a steady stream of communication. Now the King of the Gatoan Empire wishes to enter into an alliance with Earth."

"Excuse me, Sir," Jeremy politely interrupted. "I hate to ask for quickness, but my partner and I are tired from our ten-hour flight to get here. Can we keep this brief?"

Jewels changed her giggle into a quick cough at the expression on the General's face. *::Thought we were to be polite?::*

::Screw it. They want us to do a job and I've got a feeling it will be dangerous for you.::

::I can take care of myself.::

::Don't get huffy, Kid. I'm calling it like I see it.::

Jewels saw General Zenath's glare. *::Uh, Jeremy, you made him mad.::*

"Colonel Lingley, here is the "brief" version. An alien race will be here in one week to forge an alliance with us. We want your partner to test them, discretely of course, for psionic ability."

"You can't be serious!" Jewels yelped and blushed when all eyes turned to her. "Sir," she added belatedly.

"But I am, Lieutenant. Humankind can benefit from the Gatoans' advanced technologies. Our Diplomat and Intel agencies believe our new allies are withholding information. The Gatoans are very interested in humans and our psionic abilities."

"And what, Sir, did you tell them?" Jewels was sure she knew the answer and it saddened her.

"That it is rare, and when psionic powers manifest, they are small in nature, nothing earth-shattering."

::Interesting. Once again our powers are deemed insignificant,:: Jeremy growled.

::It won't be the first time we've had to play down our talents. I'm

more afraid of what the contact with the aliens' minds will do to us.::

"Colonel, Lieutenant, we want only verbal conversation from here on out," the President ordered. He banged his cybernetic hand on the desk.

Jewels jumped guiltily. "Yes, Mr. President, Sir. Sorry, Sir!"

Jeremy smoothed his expression into a blank look and replied, "Yes, Sir."

Jewels snuck a glance at her partner's face. She could see the angry tic throbbing underneath his chin. Jeremy was heading for a cold rage, the kind that scared her with its intensity.

"Now, your orders are these." The President rose and came around the desk to stand directly in front of Jewels. His focus was completely on her.

She felt the power of his will and flinched. She saw a hint of emotion flicker in his eyes. She almost backed up, needing space, but Jeremy's calm strength filled their bond and she stood firm.

"You are to be present at the landing pad, one week from today, at Fort Blackwater with the base's troops. When our diplomat greets the Gatoans you will test their mental power while reporting simultaneously via your partner. Colonel, you will be stationed inside the command center along with medical personnel to monitor the situation and keep tabs on her vitals. I expect, Lt. Enbran, a full report on your findings."

"Yes, Mr. President." Jewels was unhappy with the mission and its parameters.

Jeremy didn't seem to be taking the news any better than she, but he only cursed telepathically while keeping his expression neutral.

Jewels had a sinking feeling that they were setting something in motion that was better left alone. She knew they would regret this.

*   *   *

After the pair left, the four men silently regarded each other. The quiet was broken by the President's sigh. "Are we doing the right thing, Brion?"

Colonel Brion nodded. "We are. I know her age is a concern, but it can't be helped. She is our strongest and most gifted psionic. No other telepath even comes close to the power that young lady can wield."

"She's been indoctrinated like the others. The assignment may not be to her liking, but the Lieutenant has never failed to carry out a task. I attribute her high success rate to the anchors we pick for her," a voice interjected from the dim corner across the room.

The President grimaced and touched his cybernetic arm. "Colonel Manroe, didn't your mother teach you not to sneak up on people?"

"Well, Psi-Ops is my mother, so I will have to say the opposite is true, Mr. President. Sneaking around and unsettling the masses is *my* job."

The other men chuckled and the atmosphere relaxed.

"Leave it to you to have a witty rejoinder," General Zenath snorted and headed to the bar to pour drinks.

"I came with the updates you requested. I also wanted you to know that Jewels discovered and disabled the spybots in the other room."

Manroe took a glass from Zenath and sat down.

"How long did it take?" Hinson downed his shot of whiskey and gestured for the President to grab a glass.

"Do you mean how long for her to disable them or how long before she noticed?"

"Both."

"It took her less than thirty seconds to disable them. And as far as being aware, we're not sure if she knew and pretended not to notice. It was her partner who pointed them out." Manroe shrugged at the surprised looks of his companions. "I keep telling you, don't underestimate her or her anchor. Colonel Lingley is a dedicated and decorated Psi-Ops officer in his own right. That's why we paired them in the first place."

The President steepled his fingers and studied Manroe. "As current leader of the Psi-Ops Division, and as my friend, answer this for me. Will we regret using her?"

Manroe gave an enigmatic smile and stood. "I'll let you draw your own conclusions, Dimitri." He straightened and mock saluted the other three. "Good day, gentlemen. May all our plans come to fruition and may mankind continue to prosper."

"Colonel, wait!" General Zenath reached out a hand, but Manroe had vanished from his spot.

"I really hate it when he ripples out like that," General Hinson complained.

"I don't enjoy his cryptic words of wisdom. Makes me feel feeble-minded," Brion retorted.

"I think that is why he does it, my friends. I have nothing more to discuss." Dimitri looked at his advisers to see if anyone had anything to add. When no one spoke, he continued. "For now, let us adjourn and hope that young woman does not fail us."

Chapter 2

The enormous, oval shaped ship glided effortlessly through space, as it journeyed from the Gatoan Empire's homeworld to the Milky Way Galaxy. Aboard, the travelers bustled about, excited as they neared their destination, the planet Earth.

King Renten LoudRoar sat in the captain's chair and watched his subjects move about the bridge. He tapped his claws against the strong armrest that bore scratch marks from previous occupants. His mane was well maintained and glowed with health. His tawny fur shone from his morning grooming.

A palpable tension filled the air and it was a pleasant one to his senses. It meant alert warriors and sharp minds. He needed everything to go well. The dissidents back home advocated isolation, saying that it was safer behind their own borders. Renten begged to differ. Their mortal enemy, the Lupinous Empire, was slowly eroding away at their territory. His people had to face facts. They needed help, preferably from a species that knew nothing about them or their feud with the Lupines.

The el-lift doors whooshed open to his left and Crown Prince Dex LoudRoar strode in. His black fur rippled along his muscular form. The only sign of Dex's mixed blood was the patch of tawny fur in the shape of a star across his chest. The young male's eyes glittered with barely suppressed emotion as he came to a stop at the King's side.

"My King." Dex bowed low and then straightened. "Father, we have received the welcome message from the humans with the landing coordinates. Eight of our finest warriors will act as our royal escort when we meet them tomorrow."

"This is good news indeed, my son. And the scientists? Have they converted the schematics and data into a form our human friends can understand?"

"Yes, Father. Everything is completed and ready. They are eager for this exchange of knowledge."

Renten stroked his chin and studied his heir. "And what of you, Dex? How do you feel?"

"Sire…Father, I am ambivalent. I understand why we are doing this, but do you think it is fair to the humans to involve them with our problems?"

Renten chuckled. "You sound like your mother. She was always worried about others. Which is not," he held up his hand to forestall his son's protest, "a bad quality for a future ruler to have. Nonetheless, the Lupines would have learned of the humans eventually. We needed to get the tactical advantage first."

"Of course, Father. Will there be anything else?"

"No, my son. Go, rest, and prepare yourself for tomorrow's troubles."

"As you will it, my King." Dex bowed once more and quietly left the way he came.

Renten sat and considered his choice of ally. From the communication with these "humans," he and his council had learned much. They had technology, not as advanced as his people, yet still sufficient enough that an exchange could benefit both species. They also favored the Gatoans in form, except they were furless, having hair on certain parts of their bodies. They lacked claws but compensated by using blades and other weapons for protection. Their hands were a source of fascination for him. He had never seen anything like them before.

Yes, this alliance would prove fruitful for both species. Satisfied with his choice, he purred contentedly as they made their way to Earth.

*   *   *

Deep inside the center of the ship lay the well-guarded female sanctum. Females from the different royal bloodlines lounged about enjoying the humidity. Large wisdom trees grew throughout the area and their giant heart-shaped leaves provided shade in the artificial lighting. The gentle roar of the waterfall filled the air as its water spilled into the pool below.

In the middle floated a dais where a lithe, tawny-colored Onugrass lounged on a bed of pillows, attended by three smaller Onugrass females with slightly darker fur. Large diamonds adorned her neck and a circlet of sapphire gems sat upon her head.

Queen Rialla LoudRoar yawned, proudly displaying her sharp teeth. Idly she fanned herself. "Where is my drink? I am thirsty."

"It is coming, my Queen. And it has been prepared as per your instructions."

The Queen patted the speaker's head. "Good servant. We don't want me to be angry, do we?"

"No, no, your Majesty," the younger Onugrass stammered.

"My Queen! There is a visitor here to see you," announced a Loprofirass guard from her position by the entrance.

"Who is it?" Rialla demanded crossly.

"It is the Crown Prince."

She huffed, shooed away her helpers and slipped into the water. She swam to the north edge of the pool and climbed out, shook the water from her fur making her high and perky breasts bounce.

"Send him in." Rialla walked to her chair and lounged indolently, waiting on her stepson, Dex. He was one of a few whom she intensely disliked for opposing her marriage to the King. But Rialla always got what she wanted and becoming Queen was no exception. It had amused her when she succeeded. However, her interest was piqued. Dex would rather face a Lupine than come near her. So why was he here?

She pretended not to notice him once the Loprofirass guard escorted him inside. She heard soft murmurs of appreciation from the other females and was irritated. Mixed bloods were not uncommon, but among the Royals they were rare. She had heard all the stories of the grand love of King Renten and his Farsemiss Queen Byene. Every time the previous queen was mentioned, Rialla had to resist the urge to claw the speaker's tongue out. She was queen now, not some dead female.

Rialla waited a moment more and then deigned to acknowledge her

14

stepson. "What do you want?"

His jaw clenched. Clearly, whatever he had to ask her was distasteful. This intrigued her.

"My lady, as the Crown Prince and second-in-command of the King's personal guard, I must make sure you understand the plan for our meeting with the humans."

Irked that he did not address her properly, Rialla slid from her chair and stalked toward him. She stopped in front of him and stared pointedly. Two could play this game of disrespect.

Dex's nose flared and his eyes narrowed. "Do...you... understand?"

Several females that had conveniently moved closer to hear the conversation, tittered at Dex's treatment of Rialla.

Angry that he spoke to her like one would to a cub, Rialla loosed her claws, slapped him hard and made sure to scratch his cheek in the process. She ignored the gasps and the rise in tension as silence descended in the sanctum.

"I am Queen here! You will address me properly, Cub, or I shall report your insolence."

They glared at each other before Dex lowered his head a fraction in submission.

"Yes, my Queen. Master Chief Leftclaw wants your oath that you will not disgrace the King and attempt to leave the ship. No one, other than the King and his personal guards, are allowed planetside. Anyone violating that order shall visit Master Bravemore."

Rialla smirked. "See, my stepson, that wasn't so hard, was it?" She cooed and stroked his arm...slowly. She watched his face. There, his customary flash of contempt. He was becoming so predictable. Good for her, bad for him.

"You can tell the General that I understand perfectly. Now, run along. I'm sure a big strong male like you can find amusement somewhere." Rialla stifled a laugh. She loved taking jabs at Dex's loner status.

Stiffly, he bowed. "Yes, my Queen." He turned and stalked from the room without a backward glance.

Something had rattled the Crown Prince, for Dex's near-perfect control over himself and his emotions was legend among the people. She shouldn't have been able to get a response from him at all. Interesting. She flexed her paws and made a decision.

"Nala! Come here."

"Yes, your majesty?" The timid, smaller Onugrass ran to Rialla's side and dropped to her knees in submission.

"I have a job for you." Rialla whispered her instructions, and content with her plan, sent the younger female on her way. She purred and went back to the pool to enjoy the rest of the day.

Chapter 3

Dex was pissed. That female…that vile, vain female…was enough to drive a male to a killing frenzy. He touched his face where her claws had nicked him. That would be the last time she hurt him.

He really hated Rialla. Twenty-five seasons his father's junior, many were shocked when she became queen. Except for him. Dex knew that she was ambitious and coveted a title. After failing to seduce him, she'd chased his father and succeeded. She was spoiled, loved excess and was more conniving than any female he'd ever met. Dex avoided her for the most part, but times like today were a study in patience.

"Dex! Wait up!"

He paused for his friend and sparring partner, Vin SenseAll, to catch up. Vin's intimidating Rieyad bulk left males quaking and females swooning. Despite his appearance, Vin was kind and hated fighting. Ironic, since he came from a bloodline of fighters.

"You should be careful, Dex. I can smell your rage and her scent. What happened this time?" Vin demanded.

"The usual. I almost hit her, Vin. I was…this close." Dex sighed. "What Father saw in her, I'll never know. But let's talk of nicer things. What are you in such a hurry for?"

Vin chuckled and slapped Dex on the back. "Come see."

Dex started to protest, but Vin was unmoved. The Rieyad led Dex toward the training rooms.

"Vin, I'm not in a sparring mood."

"Good, because that's not what we're doing. Trust me, you'll thank me later."

"Promises, promises." Dex laughed and felt some of his humor returning.

His friend stopped at the last door. "Go on in."

Dex was suspicious. "Why?"

Vin rolled his eyes. "Must you ask a million questions?" He opened the door on a darkened room.

"It wasn't a million, just one. Why do you always answer my question with a question?"

"I do it to see if you're awake," Vin retorted. "Well, I did ask nicely."

"What do you," Dex was cut off mid-sentence by Vin's heavy slap to the back that sent him falling into the darkness. He landed face first on the marble floor. "Vin!" he bellowed and scrambled to his feet with a growl.

His friend stood in the doorway, a grin on his face. "Trust me."

"No! Don't do it, Vin!" He rushed forward, and Vin, with a wave and smirk, closed the door. The snick of the door lock activating earned a few rounds of cursing from Dex. "Vin, you are getting trounced at our next practice!"

Dex moved to find a light and his nose caught the musky scent of a female in heat. He froze, his thoughts racing.

A soft glow filled the area. He saw her then—beautiful tawny fur, nicely toned body and bountiful breasts. Unbidden, a growl of appreciation escaped him.

"My Prince, I am Nala. I am here to serve your needs." She sashayed toward him, her gaze locked on his face.

Dex was nonplussed. He didn't need this right now. "Nala, is it? Well, Nala, I'd love to stay, but I have duties to attend to." He stepped back, ready to bolt if she tried anything.

"Poor Prince Dex. Everyone knows about your problem." Nala missed his enraged expression. Oblivious to his clenching paws, she continued. "Maybe the other females were not good enough for a male of your strength." She reached him and trailed her paw down his right arm. "But I can do what they can't."

Dex's weary expression didn't faze Nala. She kept stroking his fur and peering up into his eyes.

"Let me be the female to mate you, give you pleasure." Her free paw stroked down his chest and headed lower. Her voice was husky with lust.

Dex gritted his teeth and caught her paw. "Stop! Find some other male to assuage your heat. I'm not interested."

Nala snarled and jerked free. Her eyes raked him from head to groin. She gaped and then mocked him. "So, what they say is true. You are not male enough from the waist down. Our poor King! He has an impotent heir," she chortled while pointing at Dex's unresponsive member.

Fed up with her behavior, he let out a belly deep snarl of rage that silenced Nala. Ignoring her fearful look, he grabbed her arm, and dragged her to the door. Unsurprisingly, it opened and he shoved her out into the hall. "Scram, guard slut."

He ignored her yowl of feminine outrage and slammed the door. He waited until her angry footfalls receded before he sat down. He had to stay focused. Dex hoped that the Earth visit would prove more rewarding than the voyage to it. With another sigh, he left the training room and sought the solace of his own bed.

Chapter 4

Jewels stared at her reflection and sighed. "I hate this base," she muttered. "No, not the base, but *him*. I can't stand *him.*"

Despite their misgivings, she and Jeremy were temporarily assigned to Fort Blackwater in the Southern Panhandle of the North Continent. Though she loved the ocean, the commanding officer, Brigadier General Maussey, was another story. She detested his demeanor and condescending attitude toward her and her partner.

Jewels knew why. While on a previous assignment two years ago, during a Psi-Ops sting of the Far Eastern HQ, Maussey was caught accepting bribes from smugglers. She had been the agent that found evidence of his guilt. He was demoted from General to Colonel for a short time and had hated her ever since.

The two knocks in quick succession followed by a pause and one hard knock, signaled Jeremy's arrival at her door. Her nerves were beginning to bother her and she automatically reached out mentally seeking the solace of Jeremy's mind and calm.

::*Jewels, easy, Kid. This is like any other op. You can do this. I will be with you like always,*:: Jeremy stated soothingly.

::*I know, but it won't be the same. They're separating us on purpose. We're missing a piece of this puzzle and I don't like it. If there is trouble, you won't be close enough to help.*::

::*I will not let you be harmed. Trust me. I won't let you fall, Kid.*::

21

::I'm glad one of us is sure.:: She opened the door and smiled tightly. She looked down the hall and seeing no one, flung herself into his arms.

He caught her easily and stroked her hair while she clung to him. *::I don't want to do this. I feel wrong. It feels wrong.::*

::I know, I have that same gut instinct. We can't disobey orders, Jewels. You know what they'll do to us, and to you, if we defy them. I don't want to end up like your partner Lenny.::

She grimaced. Lenny had been her third anchor partner and a very secretive man. It wasn't until they'd been paired for a year that his true nature surfaced. Cruel and murderous, he had wanted to assassinate the UPO Council and the President by using psionics and their powers. She was very young, only ten at the time, and her caretakers had ignored her warnings. She'd almost died at Lenny's hands before Psi-Ops intervened.

Punishment was swift and so harsh, that when it was over, Lenny had the mind of a toddler. Being wiped was a constant fear for any psionic, especially those employed by the government and military.

Jewels had been disciplined too, though her staunchest supporter, Dr. Elenora Cosmit, advised the Military Disciplinary Committee, against it. They ignored the doctor and used Jewels' vulnerability as punishment. They locked her up for two days and kept her bereft of an anchor's touch. It was mental hell for her and she learned quickly after that to be more vocal if her partner behaved strangely.

::Better now?:: Jeremy stroked her back once more.

She nodded, not trusting herself to speak. *::I'm being a wuss, aren't*

I?::

::No, just cautious. There's a difference. C'mon, Kid. We have to go. Don't want to give the good General leverage to use against us.::

::Yes, let's not,:: Jewels agreed and stepped back. She did a quick check of her uniform. "I'm good."

She closed her door and followed Jeremy to the command center. On the way he grilled her about the aliens.

"Jewels, one more time, list the eight major bloodlines."

"Jeremy, you're driving me crazy."

"Do it, please. I need to know that you have them straight. We cannot afford any missteps."

She sighed and began reciting what she'd learned from the mission dossier. "The High Ruling family is the Onugra bloodline. Next comes the Farsemi, Loporfir, Rieyad, Posaima, Mezalik, Eirarju and the Vasdji. They also have three minor houses: the Zakei, Eyriel and Hiesaro."

"Good. Now how do you tell them apart?"

"Well, they look like Earth felines," she retorted, intentionally misconstruing his question.

"Jewels," Jeremy growled in warning.

"Lighten up, Jeremy. Sheesh. I shouldn't say they are these types of felines. Rather, they resemble their Earth counterparts."

"Yes, and don't ever forget that or let it lull you into a false sense of superiority," Jeremy admonished.

Jewels snorted. "As if you'd ever let me feel superior."

He laughed and she managed a small grin. The moment of levity was broken by the returning feeling that something was going to go wrong.

The closer they got to the command center, the worse it got. This op was going to tank. She'd not had vibes this strong in years. And ignoring her gut went against her better judgment. Even Jeremy's reassuring mental touches could not quell her misgivings.

"Ah, my two favorite people." Dr. Elenora Cosmit smiled and pushed her glasses up her nose. The lovely doctor appeared anxious. "Don't stand there being glum. The aliens will be landing in twenty minutes and you both need to be ready. Jewels, go with Bella and get your sensors attached. Colonel, come with me."

Jewels sighed. Bella was always very nervous around her and that bothered Jewels. Meekly, she followed the woman and wondered what else would happen.

Elenora waited until Jewels was gone before speaking to Jeremy. "The test results are in."

He grimaced. "And?"

"Same as before. You have to face facts. The others are being brought in and the Choosing will start in four days." She beckoned for him to walk with her.

Jeremy sat in the chair she pointed to and removed his shirt. Elenora admired his chiseled chest. She never got enough of it. Grinning, she picked up a sensor, removed the adhesive cover and applied it right above his heart, the one part of him she couldn't touch. They'd become lovers two years ago, but she always felt left out. Jeremy was attentive, romantic and made her laugh, but Elenora knew that Jewels came first.

It was ridiculous, being jealous of the younger woman. Jewels couldn't help her mental condition. She had watched the telepath grow from a solemn four-year-old to a stunning young lady. And that was the root of Elenora's problem. If Jewels wasn't so beautiful, Elenora wouldn't feel like she was competing for Jeremy's affections.

She came out of her thoughts when Jeremy touched her hand in concern. "Doc?"

She laughed, embarrassed at her lack of concentration. "Sorry, wool-gathering." Quickly she applied the remaining sensors, one on each side of his head to monitor brain waves and telepathic activity. The other four were strategically placed on his back and chest to track his vitals. Jewels was being outfitted in a similar manner. "All right Colonel, the chair awaits."

Jeremy frowned, opened his mouth to speak, but his eyes went unfocused and he nodded instead. "Lead on."

Elenora led the way to the center console where Jeremy would track his partner during the ops. She smiled, but inside was hurt. He was in telepathic communication again! She knew the signs. "What's wrong?" Her words came out more curt than she meant them to.

Jeremy stopped and turned to her. He leaned in, keeping his words too low for listening ears to hear. "Elenora, maybe I should ask you that." His brown eyes searched her blue ones.

"Nothing is wrong. Everyone is tense. Brigadier General Maussey is one of Psi-Ops biggest critics. It is imperative this mission succeed."

"I know that, and so does Jewels. You have to admit, this is the biggest op ever for either of us. The Kid is a bundle of nerves. I need her to settle down. Her emotions are running high, too. Jewels can do it. She's got us." Jeremy took Elenora's hand and gave it a gentle squeeze. "Now, time to work."

Elenora stepped away as he sat in the chair. The consoles near him lit up with live footage of the landing area. Already base personnel were headed for the designated landing spot. He put on the comm piece.

"Everyone, let's make our skeptics eat crow," Jeremy stated and grinned at the cheers.

Elenora reluctantly chuckled. *I love you,* she mouthed and went to the medic station to keep track of her lover and his partner.

Chapter 5

Dex stood next to his father's seat and ogled the blue planet. It was mostly water yet its inhabitants bore no resemblance to aquatic creatures of any kind. The humans did have myths about sea people. He wondered what category they would place his people in.

"Just look at it, Dex. Not quite as beautiful as Felinia, but still pretty," Renten noted as his claws drummed against the arm rests.

"Yes, but different can be good." Dex grinned when his father chuckled. "Besides, we have more land, yet look at the advantages of having so much water."

"True, my son. Master Chief Leftclaw, every guard knows to keep all telepathic contact to a minimum, correct?"

Master Chief Leftclaw hauled his bulky Posaima body up from his seat. "Yes, Sire. Any who disobey earn an immediate visit to Master Bravemore."

"Good. Things must go right. We need these humans. Make sure the guards keep an eye out for Lupines. I want to believe we made it here first, but one can never be too careful."

"Yes, Sire." Leftclaw bowed and returned to his seat.

Dex went back to staring at the view-screen. The information they had received from the human probe had contained a wealth of information, including what the Earth's inhabitants looked like. The human form was intriguing.

Only ten minutes until touchdown. Dex felt it. Destiny beckoned and he would gladly embrace it. Grinning, he took his seat and readied for the landing.

* * *

Jewels marched quickly to her spot in the courtyard. About one hundred of the base's personnel, officers and soldiers had lined up to greet the arriving visitors. She slid in to place next to a Private who appeared to be close to her own age.

"Hi, name's Davis Blackthrone," he whispered and kept his gaze fixed firmly ahead.

"Jewels Enbran, and here comes the General," she hissed. She snapped to attention as Brigadier General Maussey paused before her.

"Special Lieutenant Enbran, I hope we can make it through this event without incident. Am I clear?"

She stopped herself from sneezing in his face. Whatever cologne Maussey wore was strong. "Yes, Sir. Crystal clear, Sir."

Jewels heard his annoyed grunt. Not that he could do anything about her response. It was textbook perfect.

::*Jewels, stop taunting him. Do you want to give him a reason to send you to the MDC?*::

::*Chill out, Jeremy. I was behaving and, besides, the good General knows it. Now, please hush, the aliens are landing.*::

"Company, attention!"

Jewels snapped to attention along with everyone present. She hated

28

this too. All this ceremony. Her curiosity made standing still a chore. Maussey was sadistic enough to make them stay this way indefinitely if it pleased him.

::*Jewels, focus, please.*::

::*Stop fussing at me, Jeremy. Sheesh, what is your deal?*:: Her anchor was being unusually uptight today.

::*Nothing, Kid. Sorry. I really need you calm and focused. Otherwise you're going to give the med computers fits.*::

::*I doubt that. Besides...They've landed!*:: Jewels stopped speaking, too busy marveling at the ship's unique design. It might be spaceworthy, but it reminded her of a cat. ::*I wonder if it's as harmless as a kitten or lethal like a lion?*:: She immediately banished that thought.

::*Good girl, Jewels. No profiling. Looks like they're emerging. Get ready.*::

::*Always,*:: she quipped assailed by the feeling of wrongness.

"Company, at ease!"

She was relieved. Perhaps Maussey would play nice for the arrivals. Jewels watched the diplomatic liaison, a short nervous man named Larry Mellen, hurrying to the ramp. He was sweating profusely and she wondered if the man's body odor would offend the aliens.

::*Jewels, I swear you think the strangest things.*::

She laughed mentally at Jeremy's exasperation. ::*I can't help it. This is new for all of us. The door is opening! Here they come!*:: Like those gathered, she was eager for a first glimpse of the visitors.

When a giant lion emerged, standing upright on two legs, no one held back gasps of awe at the sight.

::Jeremy, are you seeing this!::

::Yes, and it appears that everyone here in the command center is mesmerized as well. Now that you've ogled, back on task, Kid. You need to do the scan when they start down the ramp.::

::Jeremy, we really should have told the brass to shove it where the sun don't shine. I can't do it, Jeremy. I won't!:: Jewels felt her anchor's astonishment at her words.

::Jewels,:: Jeremy growled. *::We took this mission, we WILL finish it. No matter our personal misgivings.::*

::Jeremy, I...::

::You will obey. Lieutenant, that is an order!:: He roared at her.

His outburst rocked her to her core. Shocked and hurt, Jewels went silent. Jeremy had never talked to her like that before. She didn't know how to respond.

An uncomfortable moment passed between them. Jeremy spoke first in a calmer tone. *::Jewels, I'm here. You are not alone. If they are psionic, I will protect you. Now, get ready. They're moving down the ramp.::*

Jewels' anxiety warred with obedience, and she chose to do her job and sort out her anchor's behavior later.

Chapter 6

King Renten surveyed the humans before him. He was impressed by the different shapes, colors and ages of those present. He saw youth and the experienced.

Renten sent his thoughts and observations along the private telepathic link he shared with his son. He knew that Dex would relay them to Master Chief Leftclaw who remained on the scout ship with four of the eight guards chosen for the mission. The other four flanked him and his son.

Renten had chosen one guard from each of the major bloodlines. When the bald sweaty human cleared his throat, Renten thought it prudent to pay attention. "Yes?"

The humans' surprise at his speech amused Renten. The diplomat gaped and quickly recovered.

"I apologize King LoudRoar. We did not know you spoke Earth's language."

"We studied all the information contained in your probe. From there it was easy to adapt our translators to understand the syntax of your patterns."

The diplomat grinned. "I am Larry Mellen and I will be your liaison during your visit here. Please, follow me so we can begin the tour."

"Of course, Larry Mellen."

Larry chuckled. "You can address me as Larry. Less of a mouthful that way."

"Very well, Larry. Let me introduce my son, Crown Prince Dex LoudRoar. The others are our personal guards that will accompany us as we visit your planet." Renten watched Larry's gaze dart to a man who wore more medals than the other humans.

::He must be the leader. Make a note of it, my son.::

::Yes, Father. I do not like his scent,:: Dex growled.

::His scent is…interesting. Be careful around him. We do not need a misstep.::

::Understood, my King.::

Renten was composed. He waited for the silent byplay between their liaison and the male with the power to finish. He'd always been observant. You had to be to hunt and to lead, two things Renten excelled at. The moment passed and Larry urged them down the ramp.

They had only moved a few paces when Dex let out a telepathic roar of challenge and teleported near a certain section of the lined up soldiers.

::Dex! What are you doing?:: Renten demanded and broke into a sprint. He left behind the liaison and moved toward his son.

*   *   *

Jewels was sweating not just from the heat, but from nerves. The diplomat was funny and that made her smile. It didn't quite quell her fear that something would go wrong. She was impressed that the

32

Gatoans spoke and understood human speech. Her admiration was cut short because Jeremy was in her mind, once again ordering her to do the scan.

::For the record, I want it noted that this is a bad idea.:: She focused on the Gatoans and with her gentlest touch, reached out and brushed against the Prince's mind. She was not prepared for the reaction. She had mere seconds to realize the aliens were psionic and then the Crown Prince was before her.

::Did he just teleport?:: Jeremy shouted excitedly.

Jewels was busy studying the male before her and didn't respond. The Gatoan's glossy black fur with that odd patch of tawny hairs in the center of his chest intrigued her. And he smelled of cocoa and cinnamon, her two favorite scents. He towered over her by a good foot, if not more. She was impressed that he walked upright. Definitely different from Earth felines.

They stared at each other. All awareness receded. Tension and something more flared between them. The Prince didn't give her time to analyze the situation. He stretched out his paw, touched her face, and the impossible happened.

The bond that anchored her to Jeremy crumbled. She screamed aloud and telepathically in pain from the abrupt separation as the assault of everyone's thoughts slammed into her unprotected mind.

"Stop! Please!" she implored, disoriented while her mind tried to reconnect to her anchor. She couldn't seem to make her body obey her command to run either. She was frozen in place.

Instead of Jeremy's familiar mind, Prince Dex's mind locked on to hers and the sheer power swallowed her up like a black hole. His mind was too alien for her to handle.

Her chest heaved and her heart raced. She had to break free from his mind! But she couldn't move. The Prince had taken control of her limbs. Dazed, she watched the King approach. Jewels noticed his raised paw and knew with certainty that he too was going to read her mind. And she was powerless to prevent it.

::*Jeremy! Jeremy, please help me! You promised not to leave me! Where are you?*:: Her cries met only emptiness.

The King's paw touched her right cheek and a fresh wave of pain burned her synapses and made her nose bleed. The King removed his paw and his eyes glowed. His low purr made her shiver. "Fascinating, Dex," he murmured.

Jewels was still immobilized. Blood fell from her nose and hit the Prince's fur, but he didn't seem to notice. He studied her face once more and slowly lowered his paw. The mental hold over her vanished.

It took her confused mind and eyes a moment to realize that the three of them were surrounded by the snarling Gatoan guards and the base's soldiers. The Gatoans' claws were out and the soldiers had weapons drawn and trained on the visitors.

"No," Jewels whispered. She couldn't let the soldiers harm the aliens. Not when it was her fault to begin with. Her head throbbed and her mind was raw from the press of so many thoughts. Some instinct made her drop to one knee, head lowered in submission. She felt the King's and Prince's surprise.

"Sire, I ask pardon for the intrusion. It will not happen again." She

34

shivered and felt faint, worried that they would refuse her apology.

Jewels felt a gentle squeeze on her shoulder and then the Prince spoke, his words warm and kind, "You are forgiven, little human. Rise."

Shakily she stood and shot the Prince a relieved look. "Thank you."

He smiled and she glimpsed a mouth full of dangerously sharp teeth.

"Lieutenant Enbran! What in the bloody blazes do you think you're doing?" Maussey's bellow startled her, but it was his loud thoughts that made her flinch. She came to attention, ignoring the Prince's quizzical expression.

Maussey's face was red with fury. "I asked you a question, Lieutenant!"

"Nothing, Sir. It was," her eyes flicked to the King and then away. "a misunderstanding on my part. It will not happen again...Sir."

Jewels locked gazes with the Prince and hoped that focusing on him would help her ignore the agony of her aching head.

Maussey's eyes narrowed. "A misunderstanding? Well, Lieutenant, let's see if you misunderstand this. Report to the CC immediately. Dismissed!"

"Yes, Sir." Jewels saluted, turned and walked away, her back ramrod straight, her head held high.

Chapter 7

Jewels waited until she was close to the Command Center before letting any pain show on her face. Her mind was being scoured from the endless barrage of thoughts. Each one became a stab of torment pulsing along her blistered neurons. Whatever the Gatoans had done during the telepathic exchange had exposed her one weakness and turned it against her. She wanted to believe it an accident, but nothing could be ruled out.

The door opened and Jeremy ran out and scooped her up in his arms. "Jewels, you're trembling and you're burning up! Why did you let them touch you like that? Why didn't you run?"

Jewels didn't try to contradict her anchor. She couldn't have outrun two giant cats. Jeremy was talking too fast. He only did that when he was worried or extremely angry.

"Sorry," she whimpered, too tired to diffuse his ire.

"You should be! I swear if you were my kid, I'd tan your hide for that stunt! You almost gave me a heart attack. And when our bond was severed...." He ground to a halt, his gaze haunted.

She winced. That had been a scary moment. To know that it had affected him too, made the pain in her mind more bearable. He muttered under his breath and took her inside. She was shivering uncontrollably by the time she was put on the med-scanner table.

"I feel so cold. My fingers are numb. Doc, was wrong wit me?"

36

Jewels shook her head. "My wods are slurring. Help me." She heard her funny speech, but the voices clamoring inside her skull wouldn't shut up enough for her to concentrate.

"Jer, ake stop. Ease?" Jewels moaned and curled into a fetal position. The pain was excruciating and she closed her eyes. She could hear whispers. They were so far away....

An alarm blared and two more followed. The monitor screen lit up in several sections.

"She's flat-lining!" Elenora yelled and the medical crew sprang into action.

Jeremy was shoved back and brusquely ordered to a corner. He didn't wait to be told anything else. He stood at a safe distance, watching as Elenora fought to save Jewels' life.

He still couldn't forget the moment the Gatoan Prince had broken his bond to Jewels. He hadn't thought such a thing possible. Why Jewels? Did the Cats do it as a test of some sort? If they did, why? Or was there another motive?

The abrupt silence caught his attention. Jeremy glanced at Jewels on the table. It took a moment for him to notice the reason for the quiet. Prince Dex LoudRoar stood by Jewels' side, blatantly ignoring the weapons trained on him.

"Human healer, let me help her," the Prince offered.

Jeremy strode over and glared at the giant Gatoan. "It's your fault she's in this condition! If you hadn't broken my bond to her and left her sensitive mind unshielded, Jewels would be okay!"

"Colonel!" Elenora hissed, panic in her eyes.

Jeremy wasn't backing down. He tried to ignore the erratic beeping of the monitor that showed Jewels' falling vitals.

"He needs to know that his touch caused her injury. She didn't hurt him or the King. You didn't have to be so violent. She was just curious."

"I have been inside her mind, Human. You lie. But that is no reason to leave her in torment." Dex placed his paw on Jewels' head. Nothing happened at first, but then she convulsed and the sensors went crazy, blaring warnings.

Elenora moved to stop the Gatoan, but at a hiss from Dex, she halted.

"No closer, Healer! I am almost done." His eyes glowed and Jewels screamed, her eyes wide and glazed. The alarms stopped and a quiet tension filled the room when her body went limp. Her eyelids slowly closed.

Dex removed his paw and stepped back. "Reach her now, Human," he ordered.

Jeremy bristled at the alien's tone. He gently touched Jewels' mind and felt the familiar bond fall back in place. Her mind stirred sluggishly and he thought a little humor might get Jewels attention.

::Hey, Kid. You almost gave me a heart attack.::

::Jeremy? Is it really you? Am I dreaming?::

::Yes, it's really me, so open your pretty violet eyes and see for yourself.::

Anxiously he waited until her eyes opened. Jeremy felt a tremendous load lift from his shoulders. Then she smiled and he gave a rueful laugh. He tousled her hair and squeezed her hand.

::*Don't ever scare me like that again! Sheesh, Jewels. I swear you have no sense and I've gained at least a dozen gray hairs.*::

::*Hey, don't fuss at me,*:: she groused.

Jeremy turned to the Prince. "Thank you, for her life." He didn't understand the sharp glance the giant Gatoan threw his way. Didn't these aliens know how to take a compliment? It made Jeremy wary.

Dex shrugged. "It was only right. I must go now. Let her rest. Until the next crossing of our paths."

Dex vanished so smoothly that Jeremy had to blink twice to make sure the giant creature was gone. He whistled. "Neat trick."

"Yes, it was."

Jeremy looked down at Jewels and gaped. The expression on her face...if he didn't know any better he would've sworn it was one of longing. He shook off his unease and patted her hand. "Yes, rest would be great."

Jewels grimaced, started to object, but Jeremy stopped her by placing his hand over her mouth. He pointed at Elenora's folded arms and angry posture.

"You're right," Jewels replied meekly and Jeremy smothered a laugh.

"I'm glad you find this amusing," Maussey snarled as he stormed into the room. His entrance stifled all sound and the tension level rose.

Jeremy fought down his temper. Jewels did not need this pompous idiot harassing her. Not right now, after almost dying. "General, I was just about to take the Lieutenant to her quarters to rest as Dr. Cosmit ordered."

"Good, she's going to need it."

Jeremy stiffened, not liking Maussey's tone or gleeful expression. "Why is that, Sir?"

"The Lieutenant endangered the mission and almost caused an interstellar incident. Her orders were to be discreet while gathering intel. I didn't see that happen today. As base commander it is my job to maintain discipline."

"Sir!" Jeremy tried to interject, but Maussey bulldozed ahead.

"Special Lt. Enbran, you will appear in front of the MDC tomorrow at 1800 for a hearing concerning today's events."

"On what grounds?" Jeremy demanded, incensed that Maussey was taking advantage of their orders from the higher-ups.

"Insubordination, failure to comply with orders and intent to harm a foreign dignitary."

Maussey's smug smile enraged Jeremy. "None of those charges will stick and you know it!"

"Perhaps, Colonel. Nonetheless, she will stand before the MDC. Now," Maussey turned his attention to Jewels. "Get plenty of sleep. You're going to need it."

The command center occupants were eerily quiet after Maussey's speech. No one moved as he stalked from the room.

Jewels looked up at Jeremy with resignation and he felt his heart clench. Even if she wasn't convicted, it would still go on her record. He ground his teeth and cursed Maussey's childish need for payback.

"Come on, Kid." He scooped Jewels up. He made a note to have her eat more. She was too thin for his peace of mind. "I'll carry you to your room." He ignored Jewels' faint protest and set out toward the crew quarters.

By the time he made it to Jewels' room, she was asleep in his arms. Once again Jeremy studied her and thought how fragile she looked. Almost losing her today, and having Maussey decide to send her before the MDC, made him feel worse about the news he needed to tell her. "Two more days and then I'll do it," he muttered.

He palmed open the door and went to her bedroom. Carefully he laid her on the bed and pulled the well-worn panda bear quilt over her. "Sleep well, Kid."

He dimmed the lights and locked the door on the way out. He had to speak to Elenora about his test results.

Chapter 8

After healing the female, Dex teleported back to the scout ship. He was shaken by what had almost happened. He hadn't known how frail human minds were and the female warrior had nearly died as a result.

He wouldn't have known there was a problem if he hadn't felt the female's fear. Finding out that the mental touch of his people was harmful to her kind dismayed him. He made sure to heal her, but the encounter left him feeling guilty.

"My Prince, is there trouble planetside?"

Dex spun around and stared sheepishly at Master Chief Leftclaw.

"None that I couldn't handle." He regretted his flippant comment when Leftclaw crossed his arms and gave Dex an intimidating glower.

"Your Highness, I am head of the Royal Guard. If there is a threat, then I must be informed immediately. We can ill-afford to lose the monarch and heir on this mission. Besides, would you be willing to risk leaving the Queen in charge of the Empire?"

Dex hung his head. Leftclaw knew how to put a male in his place. He offered the Master Chief a sincere apology. "You are right and I am truly sorry for behaving like a cub. I think I should return to Father's side before I am missed."

"That would be wise, my Prince. I will be here if the need arises."

Dex gave a curt nod and teleported to a spot outside the conference room where his father, their liaison Larry, and the secretive Brigadier

General Maussey sat discussing topics of interest.

::Father, I have returned.::

::Good, my son. How fares the human female?::

::I almost lost her, Father.::

Shame hit him. It was not something his kind did. Females were to be protected, cherished—not violated or killed. Only the lowest, most disgusting beast did such things. Even accidentally causing a female's death resulted in severe punishment.

::My son, do not berate yourself. We did not know our mental strength could harm them.::

::Your words are wise, Father. But I sense the human female is more than what she seems.::

::Perhaps. We shall make inquires. Come, join me. These humans can sometimes be tedious.::

::Yes, Father.:: Dex stared at the door. Yes, the female was special to him. She just didn't know it yet. He felt more in control of his emotions and entered the room.

Brigadier General Maussey's cloy scent hit his nose and he restrained his impulse to sneeze. The arrogant human was hiding something and he really wanted to know what it was.

"My King, Liaison Larry, Brigadier General Maussey. My apologies for taking so long. I was fascinated by your architecture."

He had disliked the way Maussey had treated the female warrior and saw no need to be truthful in the male's presence. Maussey frowned and Dex smiled, baring his fangs. He saw the man stiffen.

Larry grinned. "Our base design is geared toward efficiency and defense. Our civilian homes are different. How is it for you?"

At his Father's nod, Dex answered. "We live in the forests of our world. Each grove is comprised of the different bloodlines."

"Fascinating," Larry murmured while he made notes.

"Liaison Larry, if I may be so bold. Are we allowed to meet more of your psionics?" Dex watched Maussey's fists clench and noted Larry's surprise.

"Uh, um, hmm. I don't know. I'll have to get authorization."

"You do that. After all, this venture is all about discovery. And we wish to avoid any more 'misunderstanding' like today." Dex's barb struck home and Maussey ground his teeth.

::Father, I can't read his mind. I guess he has natural mental shields, but I will watch him. People like Maussey will cause us problems later.::

::Very observant, my son. I will inform the guards as well.::

::Thank you, Father.::

Dex yawned. "I'm feeling tired. Perhaps we can speak later?"

"An excellent idea, my son." Renten stood and Larry scrambled to his feet. Maussey scowled and slowly rose.

Dex was eager to explore the base. And perhaps find that female. He followed his father and Larry from the conference room to their temporary quarters.

Larry left and the royal guards silently took their positions outside the door.

Dex and his father went inside. Dissatisfied with the day's events, he stalked over to the small couch and sat.

"I think that went rather well," Renten murmured from his spot at the kitchen table.

Dex grimaced. Trust his father to understate his dislike of a situation. "Father, I'm beginning to believe we made a mistake coming here. Do we really want to be allied with such a secretive species?"

"You forget, my son, that we have secrets too. We need the humans. I think we should try a different approach."

"Oh?"

"We should seek answers from the human female warrior. We got some information from the Touch. I sense we could gain more."

A growl escaped Dex's mouth, earning him a sharp glance from his Father. Abashed at his strange reaction to his parent's words, he surged to his feet. "I think I shall retire. Tomorrow will be an interesting day. Good night, Father." He walked to his sleeping room and closed the door.

He flopped down on the bed and scowled at its softness. He was accustomed to harder surfaces, but that didn't bother him. No, what worried him was how protective a certain olive-skinned, violet-eyed human made him feel. Troubled by his thoughts, Dex finally fell asleep.

Chapter 9

Jewels spent all day in a daze. She managed to hide from Dr. Cosmit who wanted to do a complete physical. She just wasn't up to it, not with the Military Disciplinary Committee hearing that evening, which brought on feelings of dread.

She spent the time wandering aimlessly while she tried to fortify herself for possible outcomes. She knew that no matter what, Maussey would make sure some type of corporal punishment would occur, of that she had no doubt. It was rather a matter of the severity of the punishment that he would choose that concerned her most.

She wanted to forget Maussey's eagerness to see her tried before the MDC. She was really wishing she'd never agreed to this assignment.

"Lt. Enbran, please wait up!"

Startled, Jewels stopped and turned to see who was calling her. She frowned when a brown-haired Private hurried over to her. When he got near enough for her to see his face she relaxed.

"Ah, Private Davis Blackthrone. I'm sorry. I didn't hear you. I was lost in thought."

Davis grinned. "That's all right. I just saw you and wanted to say hello."

He blushed and Jewels was puzzled. "Oh. Well, hello." She gave him a sideways glance. Enlisted personnel usually were not this formal with officers. Any other person would cite regs. Jewels didn't care for ceremony and decided not to chastise Davis for his lapse of protocol.

Davis smiled. "I also wanted to tell you that I thought you were brave to have let those alien creatures touch you like that."

She stiffened. "Private, bravery had nothing to do with it. And for the record, our visitors are not creatures. They are aliens, but their physiology is close to ours with a few differences." She recalled those Gatoan features and grace, especially the Prince's physique; very fluid and lethal, yet some gentleness underneath that predator skin. Yes, a walking contradiction.

"Lieutenant?"

"Hmm? Oh, sorry, I did it again, didn't I?"

"I wouldn't know. I think the aliens are dangerous and we shouldn't have brought them here. What if they get loose and hurt civilians?" He touched her hand, clutching it tightly in his hot grasp. "I mean, what if they are coming to enslave us?"

Davis' words earned him a glare from Jewels. She jerked hard and pulled her hand free of his. "Private, you need to get a hold of yourself. You're embarrassing yourself and the military by behaving in such a fashion," her tone was frigid, but she couldn't help it. His words incensed Jewels.

Davis reared back as if slapped. He gave her a hurt look. "I thought you'd understand."

His words baffled her and she sighed. "Look, Davis, I'm not sure what you thought I'd understand. I'm a telepath. That's why I'm used to being considered a freak, alien and a monster. I'm the last person that can cast stones at another because of differences. I have to go now. I have an appointment with Dr. Cosmit."

She wanted to get away from the Private. He was making her uncomfortable. Jewels brushed by him, intent on leaving, but he snagged her arm and yanked. Off balance, Jewels tumbled backward and into his arms. She wasn't fast enough to avoid the hungry kiss Davis ground against her lips.

::Get off me!:: She slammed the mental command into his mind and was rewarded with a howl of pain as he shoved her away from him. He stumbled back clutching his head.

Jewels staggered, found her footing and fell into a defensive crouch. "If you ever, touch me again without permission, *Private,* you will learn the meaning of the word monster," she snarled.

Davis threw her a venomous glower. "Don't worry, Bitch, I won't touch you again. Alien lover scum!" He whirled and stalked away.

She waited until he was gone before sinking to her knees. Shaken by his behavior she simply sat, trying to piece together what had caused the Private's irrational behavior. Finding none, she stood and jogged toward the north end of the base.

Jewels reached out, seeking the comfort of Jeremy's mind. If she could touch him, it would steady her. Distance, at least for her, was relative. She could 'hear' anyone she chose. She found his mind, brushed against it and hastily recoiled. Jeremy and Elenora were in the middle of some intense lovemaking. She felt her face flush.

She needed space and quiet to think. Things were becoming too complicated, even for her. She decided not to tell Jeremy about her run-in with Davis. Her anchor wasn't known for being tolerant of bigotry nor of men trying to take advantage of a woman.

*   *   *

Dimitri stood at his office window and brooded. He was taking a break from his UPO tour to rest at the European HQ building. The reports he had gotten from Fort Blackwater were not good. They hadn't expected Jewels to have such a hard time with the minds of the Gatoans. Nor for it to be life-threatening for her.

He could feel the beginnings of a migraine starting which only added to his aggravation.

"You know, Dimitri, giving the view an evil eye will not change things."

"Manroe, don't you ever knock?"

Behind him, Manroe chuckled. "Why should I, Mr. President? You, however, should be more aware. I might have been assassin sent to kill you."

"At this point I wouldn't have objected." Dimitri turned around to stare at the other man. Manroe was in his usual black and gray uniform with shades covering his eyes. "You know I don't like it when you hide your eyes."

Manroe shrugged. "Deal with it. You might be comfortable with staring at them, but I don't need you any more distracted than you already are."

Dimitri sighed. "You said she's the best and that she could do this.

So far I'm not seeing much in the way of results. I did, however, receive a request from Larry that the Gatoans wish to speak with psionics."

"Oh? Or do they have one particular one in mind?" Manroe asked with a smirk.

Dimitri paced before answering. "I get the sense that they may have our young Lieutenant in mind. Larry would have told them that she's out of their reach. I don't think that will deter them for long. I need a game plan here, Chris."

Manroe twitched and went still. Dimitri felt the heat of his gaze and it raised goosebumps.

"We have a game plan. You just have to be patient and stick to it." Chris held up a hand. "I know it's hard, but if we interfere, things will end...badly."

Dimitri flexed his cybernetic hand. "How bad?"

"Enslavement, death, loss of freedom and eventually extinction."

He felt a chill at Manroe's dead tone. "It's a strong possibility, if she fails. This is why I hate your ability. Too many what-ifs. Makes my head ache. I don't know how you even stand it."

"I've learned how. I also know that hope, love and courage are game changers. That's why if we stay to our course, we will triumph and keep Earth and its people safe."

"You've never led me astray old friend. And I'm too old to start doubting you now. I'll keep up on the news from the base. I shall agree that the Gatoans can speak to a psionic. I think Colonel Lingley will do just fine in that role."

"As you wish. I must be off, my friend. People to terrify, wrongs to right. You know how it is," Manroe joked.

Dimitri laughed. "Yes, I do know, don't I?"

Manroe grinned and vanished from view.

Dimitri turned and went back to gazing out the window. He hoped that the possibility they strove for would, in fact, become reality.

*   *   *

Jeremy lay curled around Elenora. She had found sleep, but he could not. He had been surprised to feel Jewels' mental touch during his lovemaking. Before he could find out what she needed, she was gone and had thrown up a barrier between them. She might not be able to shield herself from thoughts, but she could keep an anchor out of her head if she chose to do so.

He kept envisioning Jewels' reaction when he told her the news about his anchor status. It wouldn't be pretty and it would hurt their relationship. Carefully he untangled himself from Elenora and left the bed. He needed space. He donned his uniform and was heading for the door when his vid comm buzzed.

He cursed under his breath and hurried to answer it, grateful that it was installed in a room away from the bedroom. He wasn't prepared for the person on the other end and didn't conceal his surprise. "Mr. President!" He snapped to attention.

"At ease, Colonel Lingley. No need for formality. It is I who should apologize for calling at this time. I have new orders for you."

Jeremy relaxed. "That's good to hear, Sir. I know that Jewels and I are looking forward to getting off this base."

"Colonel, those orders have not changed. The order I'm about to give you is for you alone. Not your partner. And she is not to be made aware of this either."

"I don't understand, Mr. President." Jeremy kept his expression polite, but inside he was getting angry. Nothing good came of trying to keep one's partner in the dark.

"The Gatoans have requested that they be allowed to speak to psionics. They strongly hinted that they wanted another crack at Lt. Enbran, but I don't think so. Instead, you will answer their questions. They have a Level 3 clearance. Treat them like any foreign ambassador. Use your judgment, Colonel. Don't give them information that can be used against us later."

"Do they know they will be speaking with me, Mr. President?"

"I wanted to inform you first before having their liaison tell them. You will be joining them tomorrow for an information session."

"Yes, Sir." Jeremy nodded and waited.

"That will be all, Colonel Lingley."

The screen went dark and Jeremy glared at it. What kind of game was the President playing now? He didn't like it, but orders were orders. He left the room and paused outside the bedroom. Elenora still slumbered. He smiled. Soon he could tell her the words she needed to hear. But duty first. He left and walked toward the aliens' quarters.

Jeremy was almost there when he saw Larry hurrying toward him. "Liaison Mellen, I was told that I would be speaking with our guests tomorrow."

"Yes, Colonel. Tomorrow evening would be best."

"Now that we have that settled, I've got reports to catch up on. Good day, Mr. Mellen." Jeremy didn't give the nervous liaison a chance to add anything as he briskly strode away, his thoughts on Elenora and Jewels.

Chapter 10

Evening came all too soon in Jewels' opinion. She hated General Maussey even more for choosing 1800 as the time for the hearing. It meant that everyone on base would be privy to a broadcast of her meeting with the MDC, a fact she was sure Maussey had factored in. Everything seen during the hearing would reinforce his rule and would weigh heavy on the soldiers as they dined. They would be grateful that it wasn't them being held up as an example.

Jewels stared at her pinched reflection and tried to muster some semblance of calm and courage. She failed. She was scared. The regs gave the base commander final decision for the type of punishment meted out if the accused was found guilty. The MDC only heard evidence and voted for punishment or the dropping of charges. She had a sinking feeling in the pit of her stomach that the latter would not be her fate. Maussey wanted to hurt her for damaging his career. He would make sure she was disciplined.

She sighed when she recalled what Jeremy and Elenora were doing when she reached out, seeking the comfort of his mind. Embarrassed, she'd recoiled from the contact and had gotten angry at herself for feeling awkward. She knew what sex was. It was a normal healthy activity for adults. She hadn't liked feeling left out and she knew why. What Jeremy felt for Elenora was deep, even though the Doctor didn't know that. Jewels wanted someone to feel that way about her.

::*What if someone does feel that way about you?*:: The words were a faint whisper in her mind.

Jewels yelped, whirled around, looked for an intruder and found none. She tried to relax. "Great, now I'm hearing things," she grumped and glanced over at the clock. One hour until the hearing. Not able to take the waiting, she grabbed her jacket and fled her room for the cooler outside air.

She didn't really have a destination in mind. As long as she was away from the crew's quarters, she would be fine. The base was located on an isle and right now, the thought of seeing the ocean made her feel better. Location in mind, she teleported outside the security gates and jogged toward the shoreline.

The breeze felt good on her face. She took off her jacket and unbuttoned her shirt. Feeling rebellious, she kicked off her confining boots. Her toes sank into the wet sand and she sighed.

Jewels closed her eyes and sought the inner peace that still eluded her. She was going to need it. She had to get control of herself. Maussey didn't need any extra ammo at the hearing.

Jeremy, she knew, would try to defend her, but in this case, she didn't need rescuing. The only way to get the good Brigadier General off her back was for him to get some revenge for his loss of rank two years ago. Even if it meant a harsh punishment, she was willing to take it. Perhaps then Maussey's anger would cool and life could go on.

"Are all humans this interesting?"

Jewels stiffened and spun around. Her eyes narrowed. "Your Majesty, how did you get here?"

King Renten smiled. "I followed your scent." His tail swished back and forth. "But you have not answered my question. Are humans interesting?"

Jewels didn't know what to say. She wasn't a diplomat and she wasn't sure of the Gatoan's clearance level. Instinct told her the question was not benign.

"I suppose it depends on what you define as 'interesting,' your Majesty," she hedged. She scooped up her jacket and boots.

"In a hurry to leave my company?"

"I mean no disrespect. I have some place I must be."

The King studied her and frowned.

Jewels fidgeted under his stare. "Is something wrong, your Majesty?"

"You are different from the others I've met."

She twitched and glanced away. "Yeah, I get that a lot," she whispered. Even an alien could tell she was a freak. Her day just kept getting better and better.

"I mean that as a compliment, human female. Your mental energy is amazing and different from the color of ours."

"Colors? Wait, you see psionic energy as colors?" Jewels was surprised. "I mean, are you the only one who can?"

"No, I'm not the only one. All my people have that ability. Is it not the same for humans?"

She shook her head. "Some can see the energy, but as far as I know, I'm the only one who sees our energy in that manner."

"Fascinating. Tell me, then, what do you 'see' when you study my energy?"

Jewels caught herself before she answered the King. He was very sly with his questions. She'd almost said too much. She peeked at her watch. Twenty minutes until the hearing.

"I would love to look, but I have to go, your Majesty. Please, return to the base as well." Jewels figured that formality might get the Gatoan to follow her suggestion. She didn't need any more trouble.

Renten grinned. "I see. Maybe another time." He bowed slightly and teleported away.

Jewels sighed at his abrupt departure. "Well, I guess that's that." She cast one last longing gaze at the ocean before she too teleported back to the base.

*　　*　　*

Jeremy paced back and forth in his room, stopping periodically to glare at the clock. Twenty minutes until Jewels' MDC hearing and still no Jewels. She wasn't in the immediate vicinity and he was starting to worry.

A knock on his door brought his focus back to the present. He opened the door and stared at his visitor.

Prince Dex stood on the other side, flanked by his two guards and accompanied by Larry Mellen. Jeremy went on guard, suspicious of their arrival. He let nothing show as he politely bowed. "Can I help you, gentlemen?"

Dex twitched and Jeremy got the feeling that the big cat was amused for some reason. This annoyed him.

"Colonel Lingley, I'm sorry to intrude. I know you are busy and we are supposed to meet tomorrow, but the Prince would like to ask his questions now," Larry asked, clearly uncomfortable with the situation.

Jeremy raked his fingers through his hair. "With all due respect, I am in a hurry. However, I will answer any questions tomorrow as planned." He stepped out into the hall, forcing Larry to back up.

"I see, that will be fine, Colonel," Larry agreed and moved another step so that Jeremy could get by.

Jeremy saw Dex's eyes narrow. Oh, so the big boy didn't want to wait. Too bad. Jewels came first. "Good evening, gentlemen." He hurried away, swearing softly as he saw the time.

Chapter 11

Jeremy could make it to the hearing with only a minute to spare if he teleported there. Locking on to Jewels' mind, he appeared right next to her just as the five judges entered and sat.

::Cut it close, didn't you?:: Jewels' tone was relieved and annoyed.

::You know me, always have to make an entrance.:: He gave her a mental hug and turned his attention to the three women and two men who would hear the case. He tried a covert scan and slammed into their mental barriers. Jeremy was worried. He didn't know if any of the judges owed Maussey favors. If they did, then Jewels stood no chance.

Maussey strutted in, followed by Private Davis Blackthrone, a young man that Jeremy had met yesterday while guarding Jewels' quarters as she slept. The Private had blushed and stammered that he'd met Jewels during the visitors' arrival and had been there during the mental attack. Jeremy recognized the signs of a crush and had firmly sent the young man on his way. He studied the Private's face and it concerned Jeremy. The younger man looked smug, just like Maussey.

The bell chimed and everyone sat. All he and Jewels could do was listen to the charges and evidence that the Brigadier General presented. Jewels would have only one chance to defend herself and then judgment would be rendered. He hoped everything would go smoothly, but he wasn't banking on it.

The middle judge, a woman, spoke first.

"This session of the Fort Blackwater Military Disciplinary Committee is called to order on this day, Thursday, September 9, 2101." She glanced down at the data pad before continuing.

"The charges as submitted by Brigadier General Daryl Maussey against the accused, Special Lt. Jewels Enbran, are insubordination, endangering a foreign dignitary, and failure to comply with orders. A plea of not guilty has been submitted by Colonel Jeremy Lingley on behalf of the accused. We will now hear the evidence."

Maussey stood. "I will let the footage speak for itself."

In the center of the room a 3-d projection appeared. Silence prevailed during the playback as the aliens' landing was displayed.

Jewels sat stone-faced beside Jeremy. Even she had to admit that it looked bad, especially when the zoomed in section showed the Prince and King's reactions to her probe and the agony of their minds infiltrating hers. She grimaced and fretted. If they did find her guilty, she would be in a world of trouble. Maussey would see to it. She twitched and calmed herself as the vid ended and Maussey stood again.

"The Lieutenant's orders were to be discrete and ascertain if the aliens were psionic. A job that was supposed to be a walk in the park for someone of her telepathic caliber. Instead, her probe alerted the visitors to her actions, causing a negative reaction and a near-shooting of the visitors by base personnel who thought the Lieutenant was being attacked. Once I was there, the Lieutenant was slow to respond to my questions about what happened. Instead, she seemed more committed to giving her answers to the aliens. Thus, the insubordination and the near harm of the visitors."

Maussey paused. "Also, the Lieutenant psychically attacked Private Davis Blackthrone when he voiced his opinion, as is his right, about the Gatoans. I brought him here to swear and affirm the truth of his statements to me about Lt. Enbran's behavior."

::Jewels, what is he talking about?:: Jeremy demanded.

She tensed and scrambled to give Jeremy an answer that wouldn't set him off. *::The Private doesn't understand the word 'no,' Jeremy. That's all::.*

Jewels knew the moment her words sank in because the bond between them trembled with Jeremy's rage. *::Easy, Jeremy. Please, I need you. Don't lose it in here.::*

She felt him struggle and abruptly he relaxed. Jeremy's emotions still swirled like a hurricane in her mind. She put up a small barrier. *::I knew Blackthorne was trouble. Should have kept walking and not talked to him at all.::*

::Not your fault, Jewels. He snowed me, too. That's all right though. I don't forget bastards who like to hurt women.::

She needed to focus. Davis had finished giving his edited version of what had transpired between them.

"As you can see, she even violates the orders from the Psi-Ops which is to do no harm to a human unless your life is threatened. The Private only showed concern and he was rewarded with an attack by the Lieutenant."

Jewels stifled a sigh. She felt a headache coming on, but couldn't worry about it because she was called to defend herself. She stood.

"I wish to first apologize if my actions, which I do not think were beyond the scope of my orders, caused alarm. I used my lightest mental touch to ascertain the Gatoans' intent. I was not prepared for the strength of the psionic gifts nor the speed with which they reacted to a perceived threat. As for the Private, he attempted to harm me when I did not share his bigoted views of the visitors. We at Psi-Ops live and die by our creed. I would not violate it, unless it was a last resort."

"Lying bitch!" Davis hissed.

The younger female judge banged a gavel and gave Davis a stern glare. "You will be silent, Private, or we will have you removed."

"Sorry, Ma'am," Davis muttered.

The woman looked at Jewels. "Do you have anything else to add, Lieutenant?"

"No, Ma'am. That is all I have to say."

When the judges called for a small recess, Jewels felt her nervousness return. The decision would either exonerate her or give Maussey power over her. She preferred the former to the latter, but she would manage if the unfavorable option was chosen.

A tense silence had descended on the room and neither party broke it. After fifteen minutes the judges returned. This time the elderly man on the far right talked.

"We have reached a decision. We are unanimous. On the charge of insubordination we find the accused not guilty."

Jewels saw Maussey's scowl. She was glad to know he wasn't going to have a complete victory.

"On the charge of failure to comply with orders, we find the accused guilty. And on the charge of intent to harm a foreign dignitary we find you guilty."

"What!" roared Jeremy as he jumped to his feet knocking his chair backward.

Jewels grabbed his arm and tugged. "Jeremy, sit down," she hissed, not liking the gloating expression on Maussey's face.

"No, Jewels. This is ludicrous!"

"Colonel, you will compose yourself and sit down," the judge ordered sternly.

"Please," Jewels begged and she saw Jeremy's anger vanish.

He righted his chair and sat. He glared at everyone and Jewels wanted to comfort him. She knew Jeremy was beyond angry and nothing she could say would make him feel better.

"You will not be demoted, Lieutenant. However, this hearing and its contents will be noted on your officer record. Brigadier General Maussey, it is the decision of this court that corporal punishment be utilized. For both charges, you shall receive one flogging session. The total number of lashes shall not exceed thirty."

Jewels almost swooned. Thirty lashes? It had been a long time since that particular one had been used. Of course Maussey would pick it.

"What shall be entered into the logs?" the younger female asked, data pad out.

Maussey slowly stood and made a show of considering his decision. Jewels felt sick to her stomach with dread.

"I will lessen the number to twenty-five with one stipulation. The Lieutenant must wear a controller during the discipline session."

Jewels stared at Maussey in horror, frozen in her chair at his words. Jeremy didn't have the same problem. He was on his feet again, fists clenched so tight, she saw his knuckles whiten.

"You vindictive asshole! Are you trying to drive her insane? A controller shuts down all psionic ability. She won't be able to shield her mind!"

"Precisely. You psionics are all the same, thinking you're better than the rest of us. Well, let me remind you, Colonel, that you are part of the military and took an oath to follow our rules. If that means stripping your powers and making you human, then so be it."

Maussey left his table and came over to stand directly in front of Jewels.

She stared up at him, keeping her gaze blank.

"You will report at 2030 to the disciplinary room. No detours and no running away, Lieutenant, or you'll be imprisoned next time."

"I understand, Sir. I will be there at 2030."

Maussey watched her for a moment and then grunted. "We are done here."

"Then I call this hearing adjourned. All information has been entered into the logs and recorded," the youngest judge declared.

The judges rose and filed from the room. Maussey ushered a grinning Davis out as well.

Jewels slumped in her chair and buried her face in her hands. She fought back tears. It was happening again. Just like that time with

Lenny. Maussey had done his research and she had no escape.

"Jewels? Jewels, we can appeal this. This is ridiculous!" Jeremy crouched down next to her chair. He tugged gently on her hand and held it. "We will fight this."

"No."

"What?"

"No, Jeremy, don't bother. The more we try to get out of this, the worse it will get. Do you think he's going to let this go? Or let me go unscathed? No, he has a point to make and it will be made. I'd rather this punishment than some other horror he could dream up."

"Jewels," Jeremy stopped and gave her a helpless look.

She cupped his face in her hands. "You are my anchor, but this is one thing you can't shield me from." Jewels stood and felt her legs shake. "I think I'll go to my room. I need space. Just promise to be there with me."

Jeremy snorted. "As if they could keep me away, Kid. No, I'll be there. And don't worry. What goes around, comes around. Maussey will pay for this outrage."

She smiled, but it didn't reach her eyes. "Maybe." She squeezed his hand, slipped hers free of his, and teleported to her room. She flung herself on to the bed, curled into a ball and let the sobs flow. She knew when she was screwed.

Chapter 12

Colonel Manroe strode up the wide marble steps and into the Psi-Ops main headquarters. The weather was beautiful in Switzerland this time of year, but he had other things on his mind. Like a certain nineteen-year-old telepath on trial before a scumbag not fit to be called Brigadier General. He rubbed at his temples, aggravated by the headache that had started a little under an hour ago. He rounded the corner and frowned when he spotted Colonel Brion leaning against the wall.

"Colonel, what brings you here?" Manroe knew why, but he wanted to hear Brion say it.

"Can we talk in your office?"

Manroe grimaced. A moody Brion was worse than an angry one. He walked past the Colonel and led the way. Once inside, Manroe dropped all pretense of formality.

"Okay, Xavier, spit it out. What burr do you have up your backside now?"

"Don't start with me, Chris! This plan of yours is going to explode in our faces! I don't care what you 'see,' you're not God. You're fallible."

Chris was unperturbed. "Xavier, what bothers you more? The fact that our fates hinge on an emotion or that you, for once, aren't in control of the plan?"

Xavier snarled and pounded his fist against the nearest wall, his face red and his breathing harsh.

Chris frowned. Xavier's anger issues were becoming a problem. He would have to tackle that later. Right now, he needed him to stick with the plan. "Done yet?" He asked the other man and settled himself behind his desk.

Xavier flipped him off before he too sat. "I don't know which one bothers me more. I think Dimitri is crazy for listening to you. The medical scans from the girl speak for themselves. Lt. Enbran is out of her league and you know it."

"Do I? I told you, Xavier, have some faith. If that's too hard for you, trust my track record instead."

The two men stared at each for a long time. Xavier looked away first with an irritated snort.

Chris knew he had won this round and contemplated what he would have to do to assist Xavier. The man was miserable. Chris knew why and wanted to help, but at the moment he had to see the Jewels matrix through to completion. He would tackle Xavier's problem later.

"Fine, Colonel Manroe, you do what you want. You always have. Mark my words, one day your gift will fail you and you'll have to cope like the rest of us," Xavier warned.

"Don't worry, Colonel Brion. I already know when that day will be. Now, if you'll excuse me, I have a disciplinary session to watch."

Xavier nodded, shot Manroe a measuring look, and promptly left.

Manroe massaged his temples. His headache had gotten worse. He still had fifteen minutes until Jewels' disciplinary session.

"Might as well do paperwork," he grumbled and started in on the large pile of paper on his desk.

*   *   *

Jewels awoke and stared at the clock's neon green numbers. It was 2015 and yet she remained unmoving in bed. She had fifteen minutes until she had to face the music. She was afraid. True, she'd acted tough, but fear gnawed at her insides. Being flogged was not something she'd ever dreamt would happen to her.

"Curse you, Maussey, and the horse you rode in on," she swore. Jewels was sure the whipping would leave scars. Maussey would enjoy that, too.

Her vid-comm chirped and reluctantly she got up to answer it.

"Yes, Jeremy?"

"Jewels, you're up. Good. I'll meet you at the location. And Jewels?"

"Yes?"

"I will be beside you, no matter what. Maussey cannot keep me out of the room."

"I know, Jeremy. Thank you for the support."

"I just wanted you to know that, Kid."

"I know. Bye, Jeremy." she ended the feed and went back to her room to change.

She knew why Jeremy called. They only used normal communications when they needed to appear completely human or when other psionics might overhear telepathic conversations that were classified.

She changed into her military casual shirt and pants, braided her hair and pulled it into a bun. Steeling herself for the ordeal ahead, she teleported to the hallway outside the Discipline Room.

Davis stood outside with a smirk firmly in place.

Jewels moved to go by him, but he threw up his arm, blocking her way. He leaned in until his mouth was near her ear and his warm breath hit her neck.

"Bet you wish you had taken me up on my offer, Lieutenant"

She silently counted to ten and answered, "Not really. Both you and the alternative are like a plague; unwanted and a pain to deal with."

His eyes narrowed and he pulled his arm away. She saw his other hand coming toward her to hit her. She didn't move, only pasted a serene smile on her face as his wrist was caught inches from her.

"You're getting slow, old man," she quipped, her eyes on a surprised Davis.

"Jewels, I swear you are turning into a trouble magnet! And I'm not old. I'm still under sixty," Jeremy complained.

"True. You should stop gripping his wrist like that. You're gonna break it," she pointed out.

Davis' face was red and he sputtered a threat, which Jewels and Jeremy ignored.

Jeremy's expression was harsh as he addressed Davis. "If you attempt to strike your superior officer again, you'll go before the MDC.

Understood, Private?"

Jewels stood by and let Jeremy handle Davis. A small part of her enjoyed the Private's terror at her anchor's threat.

"Understood, Sir." Davis glared at them.

Jeremy released his wrist. "Good, boy. Now, run along. The adults have things to do."

Davis stormed off and Jewels turned to Jeremy.

"Thanks for the assist."

"You're welcome. Jewels?"

"I'm glad you're on my side," she interrupted, not wanting to give him a chance to ask about her feelings. She pushed open the door and walked inside.

The room was the size of a large conference room arranged around a fat, huge pillar. Wrist shackles encircled the marble column midway up, while ankle chains decorated the bottom. A Sergeant she didn't recognize stood a few feet from the pillar with a large bull whip in his hand.

Jewels felt hysteria stir and she strove for composure. Freaking out would give Maussey too much satisfaction.

::I will remain calm. I will remain in control.::

::Jewels? We can still call for an appeal.::

::No, Jeremy. It will only make it worse. I must do this. Maussey's a sadist and perhaps this will assuage some of his fascination with getting even with me.::

::I highly doubt it,:: Jeremy grumbled as he came to stand by her side.

70

A door opened off to their left and Maussey strolled in. His gaze raked over Jewels from head to toe and she felt soiled by it.

::*I'm here, Jewels. I'm here.*:: Jeremy's soothing words washed over her.

::*I know. I...I can do this*,:: she reminded herself, bolstering her courage and resolve.

Maussey came to a stop by the Sergeant. He held up his hand to show the controller ring and the remote to it.

Jewels flinched and Jeremy went still beside her. Being forced to wear a controller meant two things to a psionic. Either you had lousy control and had to have someone teach it to you or you lost your freedom for violating Psi-Ops' laws. The controller made you human, a fate many psionics considered the kiss of death.

"It is 2030. Lt. Enbran, come forward," the Sergeant ordered.

Jewels straightened and walked to the two waiting men. She stopped a foot away from the pair. "Lt. Jewels Enbran reporting as ordered." She snapped to attention and waited.

The Sergeant nodded. "Noted and affirmed. Lieutenant, the sentence of twenty-five lashes will be delivered now. Please follow me." The Sergeant led her away from the pillar and over to a door. "Go inside and change into the clothing provided. You can't escape because the room only has one exit, the door you are entering by. You have two minutes to come back out. Also, remove your shoes."

"Yes, Sir." Jewels went in and closed the door.

She stared at the white shift before her. It looked like a cocktail dress, except this wasn't a party. The back of the material was left wide open, giving maximum exposure to her back. Jewels removed all her clothing and slid the shift over her head. She came out and was escorted by the Sergeant to the pillar.

"You must face the column. Your wrists and ankles will chained. There is some movement, but not much. I will put the controller on you after your limbs are bound. Are there any questions?"

"No, I have none."

"Very well." He pointed to where he wanted her to stand.

Jewels moved to the spot, and faced the column. With quick efficiency, the Sergeant shackled her in place. When his hand touched her neck, she flinched and Jewels felt him hesitate. She closed her eyes and willed strength to her failing courage.

"I am putting the controller on now."

She heard a hint of compassion in the Sergeant's voice, and then the hated metal slid around her neck and snapped into place.

A thousand pricks of stray thoughts slammed into her brain and she bit her lip to stop a whimper from escaping. She worked on breathing. The painful press of so many minds was overwhelming. She could not afford to lose consciousness.

"Well, let's get on with it," Maussey ordered in a cheerful tone.

Her anger at the bastard Brigadier General gave Jewels the power to fight. She would not lose to Maussey, not now, not ever. She heard the experimental crack of the whip.

"Punishment shall commence now," the Sergeant intoned.

It was the only warning she had. She heard the whistle of air and the fiery sting of the whip impact on her exposed back. The new pain distracted her from the psionic barrage. She gritted her teeth.

"One," the Sergeant counted.

The next four blows happened so fast, Jewels thought she imagined them. But then the fire of their path across her flesh reminded her that this flogging was all too real. The silence in the room was eerie. She would have looked at Jeremy, if she hadn't been too afraid of breaking down and crying from the beating and her aching head.

"Sergeant, maybe I should get someone in here who can wield a whip. You are supposed to be the best, yet I haven't heard her make a sound."

"I am the best. I was warming up," the Sergeant growled.

Jewels almost cried then at his words. She heard Jeremy's cursing. She didn't have time to think as the Sergeant rained down seven more blows in quick succession. She gasped and her shaking legs gave way. She didn't care if all her weight was placed on her wrists. Too much pain from two different fronts were drowning her in their twisted dance of agony through her body and nerves.

The whip sang again. "Thirteen."

And again. "Fourteen."

"Harder!" Maussey ordered.

Jewels was near to fainting when the Sergeant lashed her again. This time she screamed her agony, not aloud, but mentally. Pain and fear rolled out of her as she prayed for some rescue from this hell.

Chapter 13

Dex was restless. An unfamiliar anxiety gripped him. He didn't like it or its affect on his fabled iron control. He knew the cause. The human female. Those violet eyes reminded him of Felinia's vivid, vibrant and breathtaking oceans. Sailing the water during a Felinia sunset was his favorite part of living on the homeworld. It was interesting that her eyes were that color.

"My son, are you all right?"

Dex grimaced. His father's constant concern was wearing thin and it reinforced his feeling of losing control.

"I am fine, Father. I was only thinking." About her, but he didn't let that thought slip out.

His father's unconvinced expression made Dex brace for more probing questions.

"Dex, you are my son and the heir to our empire. If you are not fit for this mission, I will remove you," Renten warned.

"Remove me?" Dex stared, surprised by this turn in the conversation. "I am fit, my King." He saw disbelief in his father's eyes. "What do I need to do to prove it?"

"It is not a matter of proof, my son. You have behaved strangely, ever since your foray into the female's mind."

"I reacted to the intrusion. I do not believe or feel that I am a danger to this mission. If I do become one, I expect to be removed immediately." Dex stood proudly. His father questioned his strength of will. He would find a way to show he still had it.

Renten sighed. "Very well, Dex. Do not think I am above removing you if the need arises."

"Thank you, my King." Dex bowed and straightened.

A wave of pain and fear stabbed into Dex's mind and he dropped to his knees with a snarl. He clutched at his head and saw his father and the two guards down as well.

"What was that?" Renten roared and staggered to his feet.

The two guards, Dipaw and Nipaw, rose and immediately checked the room for intruders.

Dex was motionless. Those emotions...he recognized the person behind them. He sprang to his feet, his eyes glowing with rage. He let out an ear-splitting yowl of challenge, startling his father and the guards.

"Dex?" His father reached for him, but Dex ran toward the door. His only thought was to protect a certain human female.

"Dex, stop right now! That is an order!"

He didn't heed his father's words and when Dipaw and Nipaw moved to block him, Dex teleported.

He appeared inside a large room, claws out and fangs bared. He noted in one sweeping glance the positions of the room's occupants. He was outnumbered, but that didn't bother him. He had eyes only for her. His little human. He sniffed the air, smelled the blood and growled when he saw her bleeding back.

"Greetings. Am I interrupting anything?" Dex snarled.

Maussey's red face and ire did not faze Dex, nor did the pompous male's next words.

"You are not allowed in here. This is a private matter. Leave immediately!"

"No can do. I am here to learn about your planet and its people. Is this how you treat each other?"

"I am sure on your world, if a member disobeys the rules, they are punished, correct?"

Dex didn't want to admit anything to the human scum, but he couldn't dispute the words either. "Yes."

"That is the same here. She broke our rules and is being disciplined as a result. I'm sure you understand how that goes."

Dex gritted his teeth. He reached out to touch her mind and was appalled at the intense agony she was in. It took him a moment to realize that her bondmate was not shielding her. He glanced over at the other male and glared.

::Why do you not shield her mind? She is suffering!::

::That is the point! I couldn't prevent this. Don't you think I would, if I could?:: Jeremy snapped.

Dex pondered that bit of news. *::Is this normal?::*

::No, Prince Dex, it is not. At least, not the controller part of it.::

::Controller?::

::Yes. It is the metal ring around her neck that shuts down and prevents all psionic activity. In effect, it makes us human. The Brigadier General is making it worse for her out of spite. And I can't do anything to help her. You think you're upset? Imagine how I feel.

I'm her partner, her anchor. She shouldn't even be here having to take this from that arrogant bastard.::

Too stunned to reply, Dex stood there, badly wanting to help, yet unsure of how to proceed. He felt his father and their guards teleport into the room.

::Father! I must help her. Even her bondmate does nothing to ease her suffering.::

::My son, I heard what the human male said. We cannot interfere.::

::Maybe you won't, but I will.::

Dex leaped out of his father's reach and sprinted toward the Brigadier General and the man with the whip. He yowled loud enough to make the men twitch as he prepared to pounce.

"No! Don't do it!"

Dex froze and glanced over at the female. Had he misheard her words?

"Please, your Highness, don't do it."

Her words were whispered and he stalked to her side. "Why not?" he demanded.

"You are better than this. Please, leave now. I don't want the Brigadier General to get you kicked off the planet."

Dex was flabbergasted. Though she was hurting, she was worried about him being forced to leave her world. Amazing, simply amazing. Her courage humbled him and he bowed his head until his face was near hers. He smelled her exhaustion, pain and terror.

"For you, I will leave. But know this, I do not consider this matter closed."

"Thank you, your Highness."

Jewels winced and he rubbed his cheek against hers. A jolt hit him and he blinked. She gasped and gazed over at him wide-eyed. He couldn't stand it any longer. He wanted to soothe her. His mind reached for hers and for a brief moment, he managed to shield her from all the mental noise.

He felt her surprise, wonder and some other emotion that he didn't catch.

"We will speak again." Dex stepped away and turned to glare at Maussey in challenge. He backed away one step at a time, his eyes on the vindictive male, until he was beside his father.

He didn't resist when his father teleported them back to their quarters.

"Dex, my son." His father reached for him.

Dex moved out of reach. "I don't want to hear it, Father!" he snarled and headed for his room, slamming the door shut. He would demand to speak to a psionic. He needed to know why anyone would be so barbaric to another. He needed information, too, about his human female. He would make good on his promise and help her.

* * *

Maussey was pissed at the Gatoan's Prince unexpected arrival. He also thought he was going to die when the big cat threatened violence. The Prince had suddenly grown silent and Maussey realized that

Colonel Lingley was telepathically explaining to the irate alien what was happening. When the King and his guards arrived, Maussey started to sweat and considered calling in his own soldiers. It proved unnecessary, however, because surprising enough, the Lieutenant asked the Prince to leave. And the Gatoan did.

There was silence after the group's disappearance. Maussey turned to Sergeant Tennyson. "Finish it."

Tennyson nodded and the final five blows fell heavily across the Lieutenant's back.

The last blows wrenched sobs from the girl and Maussey was pleased. Finally, he'd broken her. He smiled and it grew wider at the hate-filled glower Colonel Lingley threw in his direction.

"That will be all, Sergeant. Colonel Lingley, Sergeant Tennyson, you will be marked as witnesses to this disciplinary session. Lt. Enbran, you will be let go, but there are two more stipulations. One, you cannot seek medical attention for your back, and two, you must wear the controller until tomorrow morning. At that time your sentence will be complete. Sergeant, release her."

Maussey saw Lingley's mouth open to object, but the other man thought better of it and frowned instead. He didn't care what Lingley did. Enbran had been humiliated, her good reputation sullied. That was all that mattered to Maussey.

Tennyson released first the ankle chains and then the shackles. Jewels slid to the floor and Jeremy rushed to her side.

The pair of them made Maussey sick. "Tennyson, let's go. Oh, and Colonel, if you try to remove the controller an alarm will sound and the Lieutenant will be forced to wear it for two more days. Please try and restrain yourself." He chuckled as he and Tennyson left the two psionics alone.

*   *   *

Jeremy wished looks could kill. He detested that man. He glanced down at Jewels' flushed face and bleeding back. "Hey, Kid, how are you doing?"

"It hurts," she whimpered and closed her eyes.

"I know. I can't help you at all. I will get you to your quarters. Do you want me to stay with you?"

"Yes, please," she moaned and shivered.

Jeremy carefully picked her up and teleported to her bedroom. He lay Jewels down on her side before hurrying to get a towel. He wet it and came back. No one said he couldn't clean her wounds. He tried to be gentle, but Jewels still cried out several times and a few sobs escaped her.

He chucked the bloody towel into the laundry chute. Jeremy snagged a chair from the kitchen and set it up beside Jewels' bed. She was already asleep and would be out for hours as her mind tried to cope with the assault of so many minds against hers.

"We will take him down, Kid. Believe me, that scum's days are numbered." Jeremy settled down to sleep and wondered how the Prince had known Jewels was in trouble. He would have to ask later. Jeremy sighed and let sleep claim him.

Chapter 14

The vast underground cavern was dimly lit and stank of dead things and putrid water, not that the inhabitants noticed. Angry snarls echoed in the air accompanied by loud yips and barks of encouragement. Two giant combatants fought in the middle of the cavern, spurred into a great fury by the circle of onlookers.

Bonebreaker sat on his stone throne and watched, already bored with the fight. He was the current Alpha King of the Lupinious Nation, but that could change quickly. On Lupinia, things occurred daily. One moment you had power; the next you could have jaws around your neck taking your life. To rule, you had to be the toughest, strongest and meanest. And you had to bring battles.

The last few forays into Gatoan space had proven fruitful. They had captured four planets and were working on a fifth. Those Gatoans, not killed during the takeover, were enslaved or served as food for his armies. It was his spies' information that gave him his biggest break in the war. The wretched Gatoans had traveled to Earth seeking help from the humans. It was laughable, really.

"Ah, King LoudRoar. You thought to meet them first. Too bad for you that you're twenty years too late," he laughed quietly, not wanting to catch his Beta's attention. Lastbite was second in height only to him and Bonebreaker kept a constant, wary eye on the younger ambitious male.

A roar went up from the fighting circle when the smaller Lupine defeated his larger opponent with a vicious snap of his neck. He lifted his bloody muzzle, howled his triumph and plunged into the crowd. There was some shuffling and the victor emerged, pulling a struggling female behind him.

Bonebreaker yawned, scratched his muzzle and stood as the pair approached. "I declare you victor, Headslow. Go enjoy your spoil."

The males cheered the grinning winner as he dragged off his unwilling prize. The others dispersed to find food or the arms of a willing bitch.

Bonebreaker sat down again. He noted Lastbite's unguarded expression of disdain at the departing pack members. "Problem?"

"No, my Alpha." Lastbite stiffened and his neutral mask slipped into place. Bonebreaker wasn't fooled.

"My Alpha, we will be receiving a report soon from our human spy about the Gatoans' plans. Whatever has called them to Earth will be neutralized."

Bonebreaker chuckled. "You are young and dumb, Lastbite. They seek allies. We will make sure they have none. It is that simple. Now go. I find myself in need of a bed mate." His eyes glowed as he leered at the now tense Lastbite. "Unless you want that privilege?" He sneered at the other male's frantic head shake. "No? Then to avoid that honor you'd better bring me news that will keep your backside safe."

"Yes, my Alpha." Lastbite dropped his head in submission.

Amused at the hate shining in his Beta's eyes, Bonebreaker left his throne, stalked to the younger male and put his nose an inch away from Lastbite's throat. "Don't try to betray me, whelp. They didn't give me my warrior name as a joke." He smelled Lastbite's embarrassment and fear. He licked Lastbite's neck slowly and growled against the Beta's bared neck. He stepped back and headed for his harem's quarters. Time to work off some of his lust.

*   *   *

Rialla lounged on the divan, her tail swishing back and forth. They had been in orbit around the planet Earth for several days and Renten hadn't bothered to grace her bed or accepted any of her comm calls. She was bored, in heat and peeved by the lack of attention.

In fact, her husband hadn't mated with her in weeks. She was confident that he didn't know her secrets or her plans. And she wondered if maybe he was slinking away into some other female's bed. That thought angered her and her tail swished back and forth harder.

The door chimed and her attendant scurried to answer. Rialla heard the rumble of a male's voice. She perked up and smoothed her paw down her fur. She'd just finished her bath and the brushing had left her with a nice silky sheen.

The attendant returned, not with Renten, but with a lean Mezalik in tow. Rialla straightened, her eyes narrowed.

"Get out! All of you." She ignored the hasty scramble of her attendants as they rushed to do her bidding.

Assured that they were completely alone, she sauntered over to the male. "I see you've lost weight, Lord Fearnone. Not as much unrest to

83

stir up business?"

Her visitor snorted. "There is always business to be had, my Queen."

"I pay you for information. So what do you have for me?" Impatiently she tapped her foot.

"It seems that the Crown Prince has a new interest."

"Really? Do tell?" This would be good. Something to hold over Dex's head.

"A certain human female has earned hands on treatment from your stepson."

"Hm. How hands on?"

"He healed her. She was dying and he saved her life. He also interrupted a discipline session to try and save the female. And the most intriguing tidbit—the humans have psionic abilities."

"What! Do they know of ours?" Rialla demanded even as she plotted how to use the news to her advantage.

"I do believe so. What would you like me to do, my Queen?"

"Go spy on her. Find out what my dear stepson sees in her. If necessary, make sure she dies and he takes the blame. Anything that discredits him before his father and our people is a bonus. I assume this will cost your usual fee?" She stretched and her breasts bounced a little.

Fearnone's nose twitched and Rialla bit back a laugh. Males, so typical, thinking with their members and not their brains.

"Yes, standard fee," his voice grew husky, his heated gaze devouring her.

She preened under his scrutiny and stroked his fur. Soon Rialla would tremble beneath his skillful hands, but not before her own lust had built. "Come, my favorite hunter, enjoy your reward." Fearnone obediently took Rialla's paw and let her lead him away.

Neither saw Nala hurry from her hiding place and out a side door.

*　*　*

The sun shone brightly, but Dimitri felt no warmth. He'd received the latest reports from Manroe and he was incensed. Dimitri had served through two wars, the American-Eurasia War and the Great War of 2086, but never had he seen so much corruption and misuse of power stem from one man.

The door chimed and Zenath and Hinson entered followed by a morose Brion. Dimitri frowned, checked the calendar and realized that it was Thursday. Every Thursday, he met with his top advisers for status updates on the various military and psionic operations going on worldwide.

"Gentlemen, please have a seat. Has anyone seen Chris today?"

Everyone shook their heads.

"Figures, he'd be late," Dimitri grumbled.

"Mr. President, I'm sure he'll pop up," Zenath assured him.

"I know, Derek, but I don't like his sudden appearances. Very distracting."

"I agree. Such a pain," harrumphed Hinson.

"You're jealous that you can't pop in and out like that, Terry," Brion

85

chided the older man.

"Calling the kettle black, aren't you, Xavier?" Zenath rebuked.

Brion shrugged. "Maybe."

"Regardless of his arrival method, we need to get started," Dimitri sternly reminded his friends. "Now, what is the progress from the shipyards?"

"We are ahead of schedule. The crews have been in training for the past six months and are eager to show off what they've learned," Derek answered before glancing down at his data pad. "Weapons testing, too, is farther along than we'd hoped to be."

"That's welcome news indeed. Xavier, what's our status with the internal investigations?"

"All agents are watching the intended targets and will be prepared to move in and apprehend all suspects. Maybe after this cleaning of house, we can all relax."

Dimitri gave a tired smile. "Perhaps, we'll see. Terry, how is the PR campaign faring?"

"All ideas have been implemented and ready to be fed to the news stations at your command."

Dimitri leaned back in his chair. A sense of relief hit him. They were in the homestretch. They only had to make it through September 22 and then they would be in the clear.

The door chimed and everyone glanced at it in surprise. It opened and Colonel Manroe strolled in.

"Well I'll be a monkey's uncle!" Derek gaped at Manroe's ordinary entrance.

"What, no fancy arrival today?" Xavier taunted.

"We have a problem."

Tension filled the room and Dimitri stood. "We do?"

"Yes. The Gatoan Prince's actions from yesterday have changed the scenery."

"What!" shouted Zenath.

"You're kidding right?" Hinson frowned.

"I told you!" Xavier crowed.

"Silence!" Dimitri roared. He focused completely on Manroe. "Chris, this had better be a joke. We set everything up according to what you saw. If it's changed then we're screwed."

Chris reached up and removed his shades. The others gasped. His eyes were glowing.

"I am telling you, the scenery has changed. Our little problem has taken a giant leap forward and will be arriving on the 11th. We're out of time."

"Dangit, Chris, your timing sucks," Terry complained.

"You'd better be glad everything was ahead of schedule or we'd be taking a serious butt-kicking," Derek pointed out, clearly unhappy with the latest turn of events.

Dimitri couldn't blame his advisers for being pissed. He was still stunned that Chris' vision had been wrong.

Chris slid his shades back on. "I've told all of you, a thousand times if not more, that what I 'see' can and does change. Be thankful that I got you the warning that I did. Otherwise, we'd be up a creek without a paddle. I have to get going. I have to pull the psionics in that we need. You'd better put a rush on all related projects as well. And may destiny have mercy on us all." He stomped from the room and slammed the door.

The quiet lasted for a few minutes as each man pondered the implications of Manroe's news. Finally, Dimitri broke it. "Okay, he gave us a day and half warning. Put in overtime, our budget can cover it. I refuse to go down without a fight. Gentlemen, let's make this happen."

"Yes, Mr. President!"

They stood and filed out of the room. Dimitri waited until they were gone to fling himself into his chair. He picked up the picture frame that sat on his desk. He traced the delicate features of the woman's face. "Patricia, I will keep my promise." He gave the photo a loving tap before setting it aside. Time was of the essence. He had vid calls that needed to be made.

Chapter 15

Jewels was having a bad day. She'd overslept and missed breakfast. The controller was removed and she had breathed a sigh of relief as Jeremy's shield fell into place around her mind. Then Elenora had pounced and she was forced to endure two hours of comprehensive and humiliating medical exams. It was the sympathy in Elenora's eyes when she saw the welts that made Jewels want to crawl back into bed and hide. If the Doc said, 'only one more', one more time, she was going to scream. Grumpily, she lay on the med-scanner bed and counted to one hundred in several languages.

She felt Jeremy coming and she prayed for a quick rescue from the med-center. That hope died when she got a good a look at her anchor. Hadn't he slept? His clothes were rumpled and his hair mussed. Jewels took a sniff and sneezed. Yep, he'd been drinking too. She studied him from across the room and pondered what it all meant.

"Can I help you, Colonel?"

Jewels winced at Elenora's icy tone. Oh boy, Doc was mad. That meant hell for someone other than Jewels. She felt a little bit sorry for her partner, but better him than her.

"Yes, you can, Doc. You can make the test results vanish."

Jewels' eyes went wide in surprise. "Test results?"

Jeremy jumped, flushed and hurried to collect his thoughts. "Jewels-uh-hi."

Suspicious, she sat up. "Uh, what, Jeremy? There's something you're not telling me. Just spill it. I'm a big girl, I can take it." She was his partner. She knew his body language and, right now, it was telling her he was beyond worry, more afraid. If anything could shake Jeremy, it was cause for concern.

"Jewels... A little help, Doc."

Elenora moved away from his side. "Tell her. That's an order, Colonel."

Jeremy scowled and Jewels tensed. He ran his hand through his blond hair. "Jewels, the tests for my anchor fitness came in."

When he paused, Jewels glared. "Spit it out already!"

"I can't be your anchor anymore. I should have stopped two missions ago, but you needed me. I did it against Doc's orders."

Jewels was aghast at his words. Tears pricked her eyes. That meant every time that she'd used her own abilities, she was destroying his. "Oh, Jeremy! Why didn't you tell me?"

"Kid, I needed your focus and having my powers break down would have been a huge distraction. I made a judgment call. Besides, the candidates all arrived yesterday for The Choosing. We," he pointed to Elenora, "decided to do it this way to minimize stress for you."

Jewels laughed bitterly and choked down a sob. "Minimize stress? You sound so clinical! At this moment, I despise you, Colonel!"

"Jewels!" she heard him shout, but she ran from the med-center.

She tried to stop the tears of hurt from falling and failed. A tightness formed in her chest. Always before, her anchors had been eager to leave when the breakdown started. Jeremy knew what to expect, what signs to look for. Why did he wait so long?

"Stupid, Colonel," she muttered and slowed to a walk. She angrily wiped away her tears. She had to get a grip. She had to be strong during the Choosing.

::Do you always have to be?::

Jewels froze. She knew that voice! She glanced about for Dex.

::Little human, do not fear me. I came to apologize.::

::Apologize?:: Jewels was confused. What did he need to apologize for? She felt his amused chuckle tickle her mind and it stirred her heart.

::You are indeed very fascinating. Look behind you, little human.::

Jewels heard his steps. Dare she turn and stare into those emerald green eyes? Eyes that promised her things that were denied her. Why him, why now?

His scent teased her nose and the air whooshed from her lungs. She had to see. She did a slow turn and stilled. Today, Dex wore something similar to a Scottish kilt. It did nothing to calm her racing thoughts.

His muscles were defined and powerful. His fur begged to be stroked and rubbed against.

"Oh," Jewels whispered, embarrassed that she was ogling the Crown Prince of the Gatoan Empire. She couldn't seem to stop herself.

Dex's eyes glinted with mischief and other things. This female was different from any other. So fragile, yet he'd seen her soul and knew her purity. He was fixated on her.

"Am I pleasing to you?" He surprised himself, and her, by asking. But it was true. Dex had to know.

She gulped and managed a breathy, "Yes."

He grinned and moved closer. "I want to touch your...skin. So different from fur."

"Yes," she agreed, her mouth dry. She wanted to touch him, too, and bury her face into his fur.

"Little human, you are unique." He touched his paws to her face and felt a slight shock at the contact. He ignored it and enjoyed the smoothness of her skin.

His touch was electric, literally. She felt the jolt and then everything went quiet in her mind. An inner voice warned her that they needed to stop, but Jewels wasn't listening.

"Dex." She raised a hand to touch him and paused, uncertain if he would welcome it or not.

He smelled her growing arousal. He saw the hesitancy. Did not females here take what they wanted when the heat raged in them? Dex took her hand, felt her stiffen and waited for her to relax before placing it on his chest. He purred when her fingers tangled in his fur and she caressed him. He looked in her eyes, eyes that had changed color to the emerald green of the forests on Felinia, and saw that intense longing. That hungry need.

Dex was confused. She shouldn't be this desperate if her bond-mate was taking care of her. He frowned and Jewels flinched. She dropped her hand and backed up, breaking the connection.

"We shouldn't! I, I can't. Please forgive me!"

"Wait, little human!" Dex called, but she'd run away. Frustrated, he glared at his paw as if it could provide some insights. He decided it was time for some answers, especially about her. Dex was sure that their liaison, Larry, would have the information about the female human. Satisfied with his plan, Dex teleported back to the complex he shared with his father and the guards.

::*Father, is Larry with you?*::

::*Yes, we are discussing the technology sharing rights. You are agitated. Has something happened?*::

Dex reined in his emotions. He had more self-control than this.

::*I am sorry, Father. I need a question answered by the human.*::

::*Come join us, my son. I need the company and we shall find the answers you seek.*::

Dex teleported inside. He grinned savagely when Larry twitched in his seat. "Now, Human, I'm tired of waiting. You will tell me about your psionics and more specifically about the one called Jewels."

Larry gulped, looked frantically around and drummed his fingers on the table. "It's not that simple, your Highness."

Dex glared and loosed his claws. "And why not?" He ignored his father's mental command to stand down.

"She is part of the Psi-Ops division. They are notoriously hard to work with and trying to get them to release information on any of their people is nil."

Frustration hit Dex and he resisted the urge to drag his claws down the nearest wall.

"We were granted permission to speak with Colonel Lingley. He will be by later this evening. If you could wait until then," Larry stated calmly.

"No! No more waiting. I wish to speak with him now." Dex ordered.

Larry grimaced, smoothed away his expression and smiled politely. He stood. "I'll go get him, your Highness." Larry hurried from the room.

The moment the door shut, his father turned to him with a thunderous expression. "What do you think you are doing, Dex?" he demanded.

Dex winced at his father's tone. "I cannot stand it any longer, Father. You saw her back, felt her pain. And for what? Because that disgusting Brigadier General carries a grudge and must get his pound of flesh?" He paced and remembered all too well how pale and fragile Jewels had looked. Yet, Dex felt pride and amazement at her strength of will. She had not budged when she asked him not to interfere. The little human female was fierce like an Onugrass.

His father's grunt caught his attention.

"My son, need I remind you that we must have humans as our ally if we are to live? Please, Dex, control yourself," Renten cautioned.

"I will do my best, my King." His ears picked up Larry's returning footfalls and those of the Colonel. Dex composed himself. The Colonel was not as easily intimidated like their liaison

"They are here."

His father nodded and returned to his seat as Larry and Colonel Lingley entered. Dex settled into a chair, ready to get some answers.

"King Renten, Prince Dex, may I present to you, Colonel Jeremy Lingley." Larry moved aside and Jeremy stepped forward and bowed.

"Your Majesty. Your Highness. I do believe you have questions for me?"

Dex regarded the psionic and felt a pang of jealousy. This was Jewels' bond-mate. He wanted to rip Jeremy apart. How could a bond-mate allow his female to be harmed by such filth as Maussey?

He didn't realize he was growling until his father hit him with a mental punch.

::Dex! You are embarrassing our people by this unseemly behavior. Stop at once or return yourself to Master Chief Leftclaw and our ship!::

::I am sorry, Father! I can't fathom why this male did not protect his mate.::

::My son, we do not know their ways. Do not condemn unless you have all the facts.::

::Yes, my King.::

Dex settled instead for glaring. "Tell me, Colonel, are human males always this barbaric toward the females?"

95

"Dex," Renten warned, his tone filled with disapproval.

Jeremy appeared pained before finally replying, "No, this is not our way."

"Tell me why, Colonel, she is different. Why did you allow that other man to harm her?"

Jeremy swore. "Look, it wasn't my choice, believe me. He covered all the bases with his charges and evidence. Jewels didn't have a chance. I can't go against the Military Disciplinary Committee."

Dex saw the other man's anguished expression.

"Do you not have any say in the process? You are her mate, are you not? In our society, punishment is left to the mate to dispense."

"Mate?" Jeremy sputtered, blushed and coughed hard.

Dex glanced at his father who shrugged. It took a moment to sink in that Jeremy wasn't coughing. He was laughing. Dex scowled.

"What is it you find funny, Human?"

"I'm sorry!" Jeremy gasped and got control of himself. "That was rude of me. You took me by surprise. Jewels and I aren't lifemates. We are partners. She is like a sister to me. Besides, I already have one I wish to have as mate."

Fierce joy sang in Dex's soul at Jeremy's words. So, his little human was mateless. That was good news for him.

"Excuse me, Colonel. I was told that the Lieutenant was not to be discussed," Larry interrupted.

Dex decided that throttling the liaison would improve Gatoan-Human relations tremendously.

Jeremy shrugged. "Our President told me to answer all questions up to clearance Level 3. That allows our guests to know about her."

"Very well," Larry grumbled and sat down.

"Any other questions?" Jeremy glanced from Dex to Renten.

It was Dex who responded. "Just one. Why did our mental touch hurt her?"

"We're not sure. It was the first time that's happened to her. We are assuming that your minds are stronger than ours. Also, we think that Jewels' disability played a part. It really wasn't any one reason."

Dex pondered the Colonel's words. "Disability?"

"Yes. She is unable to shield her mind from any living thing's thoughts and emotions. That's why she has a partner like me. I'm an anchor. I can extend my natural mental shields around her mind."

"I see. I appreciate your honesty, Colonel. I wish to know her better. How might I go about speaking with her?"

Jeremy blinked, clearly taken aback by Dex's request. He grew thoughtful. "Well, I'm about to retire from my position as her anchor. In two days, we will hold something called "The Choosing" where Psi-Ops does a series of three trials to test the fitness of potential anchors. The contender with the highest score and best emotional connection with Jewels becomes her new anchor."

"Interesting. Thank you, Colonel, for your time."

"Jeremy."

"What?" Dex gave him a baffled look.

"You can call me by my first name: Jeremy. I owe you for yesterday evening. Whatever you did helped her make it through the...session."

"I could not let her suffer," Dex admitted.

"One more thing, your Highness. The Choosing is open to all psionics. Just something for you to keep in mind," Jeremy added.

Dex grinned. "Thank you, Jeremy, I will remember."

"I have to go. If you have any more questions, have Larry page me and I'll do my best to answer them."

Renten stood. "You've been more than helpful. Your information has been insightful. Thank you."

Jeremy bowed again and left with a smile.

Dex stalked over to Larry. "I would like to speak to your President. I think it's time that we show humans how we Gatoans like to play games."

Chapter 16

Maussey was furious and didn't care that his staff cowered at their desks. It was rather easy to set Lt. Enbran up for what would have been a spectacular fall. At least, it would have been if those stinking aliens hadn't arrived. Now all his plans were in danger of unraveling. He would not let that happen.

"S-Sir?"

"What?" he barked, thrilled to see fear in Private Blackthorne's eyes.

"Sir, Lt. Enbran met with the Gatoan prince."

Maussey's glower disappeared. He started to smile and Davis looked ready to wet his pants. "Don't just stand there, boy! Report!" He listened with interest and chuckled when the boy finished.

"So there is an attraction. Not surprising, one freak calling to another. Private, continue shadowing her. I want to know her every move. And, Private Blackthorne?"

"Sir?"

"Don't fail me."

Blackthorne gulped, eyes wide. "I won't, Sir!"

"Dismissed." Maussey turned and walked to the surveillance wall. A hundred small-sized windows showed security footage around the base. He studied the wall for a moment before turning to the Sergeant

99

manning the vid console.

"Controller, I want you to tag Lt. Enbran's psi-implant signature and track it. Display her activities in Window Thirteen and keep it active at all times. I want to know if she so much as sneezes. Record everything. Find someone to tag our visitors. I don't trust them as far as I can throw them."

"Yes, Sir!"

Pleased with his plans, Maussey left the HQ building. He had another appointment to keep. This one he didn't relish. He slid into his private grav-car and headed to the city. An hour later he arrived at his destination. The area was known to be dangerous, but he was unafraid. He locked the vehicle and went to a rundown building with peeling green paint.

He checked to be sure no one followed. He entered his pass-code on the id pad and hurried inside. He closed the door and was swallowed in darkness while the security scan swept him from head to toe. It shut off and glow lights came on overhead. It was not enough for anyone to see by and that was the point.

"Well, well. Look, the good Brigadier General has seen fit to join us."

Maussey snorted. "At least I don't hide in the dark."

"True, but you are human. You bring news of the girl, yes?"

"Yeah. Everything is happening as you predicted."

A low growl echoed from the shadows. "Liar. I smell the lie on you. What has happened?"

Maussey tensed. He needed to tread carefully. "The Prince has caught her attention. She's starting to be fixated on him. I'm trying to contain the situation, but the Gatoans are psionics. You didn't tell me that. No one knows the strength of their powers. If you have information I can use, then I can be more effective in carrying out your wishes."

"I gave you what you need, use it! Or do you wish to join your fellow human failures in hell?"

Maussey started to sweat. "No, Master."

"You humans want wealth, power, and glory without working for them. Foolish children. I know the Choosing ceremony starts in two days. I will be there and claim her for my own. My enemies will never know what hit them."

"Of course, Master," Maussey murmured. He only bowed and scraped to obtain his goal. Soon they — Lt. Enbran, the Gatoans and his dark Master— would bow to him.

"Go, my slave, prepare for my arrival. And do not worry. Your unwanted guests won't know what to do."

His master gave a hair-raising laugh and Maussey didn't move until the footfalls ended and the lights came up to full illumination. He looked at his watch and swore. The door behind him opened and he hurried back to his grav-car. He would get to the base with ten minutes to spare. He drove away. A pair of glowing yellow eyes watched him leave and a sinister laugh filled the evening air.

* * *

Jewels paced back and forth. Her grief and confusion had

mellowed somewhat, but she felt blindsided by the day's events. It was barely early afternoon. Hurt, too, that Jeremy hadn't confided in her about his deteriorating condition. She could have killed him with her powers! And then what would she have done?

"You're such an idiot!" she shouted. If that wasn't enough, she couldn't stop thinking about Dex and the feel of his fur, his unique smell, his gentleness.

Jewels groaned and rubbed her arms. She'd heard of lust and passion and taken the required sex education classes too. She even tried sex once or twice. What she felt around Dex defied imagination. He made her feel flustered and her heart race. Even her thoughts about him caused an ache in her that needed to be sated.

She shook herself. "What am I doing?" she grumbled. "Can't stand around daydreaming. Besides I need to talk to Jeremy." She changed her clothes, resolutely left her quarters and followed her mental link to him.

She found Jeremy at the mess hall. She scanned the crowded room and saw him in a corner nursing a beer. This wasn't an ideal place to speak, but time was of the essence. She headed toward him and stopped a foot from the table. "Can I join you?"

Jeremy glanced up and Jewels felt guilt hit her. Her anchor looked exhausted and his eyes were bloodshot. "Jeremy?"

"Sit, sit. People are staring."

Jewels plopped into the seat and her well thought-out apology went out the window. "It's me. I'm doing this to you. You have to stop anchoring me. Doc can sedate me after each phase of the Choosing.

She..."

"No, Kid. I've not been relieved of my post. Only a coward would let you suffer."

His angry scowl made her mad. "We're talking about your life too! Do you want to end up brain-dead?" she hissed.

He chuckled, but only sadness filled his gaze. "Listen, Kid. We all die sometime. The lucky ones get to choose how to go. If I die while keeping you safe, then I will gladly do so. You don't understand how special you are. And," he put a finger to her lips, stopping her objection. "One day someone will help you see that. Now, grab some food. We have to review what will happen during the Choosing."

::Jeremy, I'm sorry!::

He tousled her hair. *::I know, Kid. So am I. I knew you would worry. I wanted to find you a worthy anchor. Aw, Jewels! Don't cry. Be tough for me, Kid.::* Jeremy blocked her from prying eyes while she got control.

"I'm ready." Her tone was lifeless. She needed to not feel. It was the only way she could cope with being parted from her best friend, mentor and partner.

Jeremy sighed. "Jewels, let's go."

She fell in beside him, tried to touch his mind and was rebuffed. Miserable and confused, she hoped they could sort it out later.

*   *   *

Lastbite hurried through the tunnel, his mind on the news his spy had sent. If the Lupines hoped to gain dominion over the Milky Way sector and enslave the humans as well as the Gatoans, they had to get the female that everyone was vying for.

His spy, nestled within LoudRoar's inner court, had informed him that Queen Rialla planned to have the human female assassinated and the crime blamed on the Prince. Lastbite wasn't going to tell his Alpha. No, the time had arrived for him to make his move.

Lastbite slowed as he neared the central den and Bonebreaker's throne. He hesitated in the opening and watched his Alpha pummel a pack member. Lastbite winced at each blow and was glad it wasn't him. Finally, Bonebreaker stopped and the unconscious male was dragged away.

Bonebreaker stood, his back to Lastbite. "You'd better have good news for me."

"I do, my Alpha. We have a chance to steal a prize from our enemies and bring them to their knees." Lastbite came fully into the room. "The Prince has fallen for a human female. If we capture her, he will follow."

"How do you plan to do this?"

Lastbite ignored the warning in Bonebreaker's tone, too excited by his own scheming. "It is rather easy. One of our human agents has infiltrated the base where the girl is kept. She is a mind reader, my Alpha. A very strong one. She is treated like an Alpha. There is to be a choosing of a new mate for her. I am confident our spy can win her. He will then bring her to us."

Bonebreaker turned, his eyes on Lastbite. "It seems well thought out." He moved closer.

"Yes, my Alpha. It is. I will make those mangy cats beg for her life." Lastbite laughed evilly and didn't see Bonebreaker's fist until it connected with his jaw and he went flying. He crashed into the stone table and lay there moaning in pain. He gasped for air and, with every pained breath, his ribs throbbed. "Why?" Lastbite wheezed.

Bonebreaker came and stood over him with his fangs bared. "There is no 'I,' Lastbite. You do all things for your Alpha and the pack. Or, maybe, you wish to challenge to be Alpha?" he elongated his claws and growled.

Lastbite frantically shook his head. "No, no, no! My Alpha, forgiveness! Forgiveness!"

Bonebreaker stuck his muzzle in Lastbite's face. "Next misstep and I rip your head from your shoulders. Now, get out of my sight. And don't come back without the female."

"Yes, my Alpha," Lastbite squeaked. He stayed still and only got up when he was sure Bonebreaker was gone. He would find a healer first. Lastbite couldn't do anything until he was fit. Then he would take some of their ships and go to Earth. It was time to show their resolve, strength and power to the cats.

Chapter 17

Dex strolled along the walkways of the base flanked by his Onugra guards, Nipaw and Dipaw. What he really wanted was to be with a certain female. As if conjured up by his thoughts, he caught a whiff of that sweet aroma that was hers.

He changed direction and made a beeline for the northernmost corner of the base. He paused when he saw the garden. The bright flowers seemed out of place against the dull colors of the base. Sitting in the middle of the plants, surrounded by the little creatures called birds, was Jewels.

Dex was sure a human wouldn't have noticed her, she sat that still. Even her psi-energy was quiet, almost suppressed. If he hadn't caught her scent, he would have missed her.

Yet, he did know her scent and it intoxicated him. He cleared his throat and the birds scattered. He was amused by the annoyed glare Jewels gave him.

"Do you mind? I was trying to have a peaceful moment."

"I do mind. You should not be left alone. I do not trust the people here." Dex crossed his arms and gave her a look meant to intimidate her into listening to his advice.

Her stern expression softened. "Your Highness, I am fine, I promise you. No one bothers me here." She stood up and dusted her pants off.

His eyes tracked her every movement. None of her actions were wasteful. She was like his kind, tightly coiled and alert to the surroundings. "Are you sure you don't have Gatoan DNA?" he joked, wanting to see her smile.

Jewels snorted instead. "I highly doubt that. We just met your kind. How could we have any of your DNA here? Unless you lied and you've visited us in the past?"

Dex, impressed with her quick retorts, moved closer until he was only inches from her. His little human was very much in heat. Idly, he wondered if humans knew the mating signs or was his human somehow different. He considered what to do. He knew he was the one for her. He wanted to bask in her heat and make her yowl her pleasure at his skills.

He reached out and stroked her face with his paw. Her eyelids closed and her breathing became ragged. Her arousal filled his nose and he took in a big gulp of air just to savor it.

"Ah, Jewels, you are so precious to me. Little Human, may I sample you? Let me drink of your sweetness, little one."

"You say the strangest things, your Highness," Jewels murmured as a pink flush spread across her cheeks.

Dex heard her sigh wistfully as she stepped away from his paw. She turned her back to him and it angered him. Here was another female, rejecting him.

"Don't turn your back on me, Jewels." he snapped and stepped up to her.

She gasped and spun around, putting them face to face. "What do you want from me?" she demanded. "I don't understand you," she added in a whisper.

Her confusion gave him pause. Why was he being aggressive with her? Was he that out of control?

"I am sorry. Perhaps I should go." Dex turned to leave, but froze when Jewels flung herself against him, her arms wrapping around his waist.

"No! I mean...please. Please don't leave me." The heat of her breath stirred the fur on his back.

Stunned he didn't move at first and then, awkwardly, he turned and placed his paws around her in a hug. "I am here. I will keep you safe," he rumbled as he started to purr. He stroked her hair and stopped to consider the object in her hair.

"What is this?" he asked and touched it.

She laughed. "It is called a hair tie. Humans use them to move our hair away from our faces so that we can see or work more easily."

"I don't like it. Can you remove it?"

"You want to see my hair down?"

"Yes, I want to see you without restrictions."

Her warm breath tickled his fur when she huffed. "For you, your Highness, I will do this. I usually keep it up." She reached behind her head and with a quick tug, let her hair fall free.

Dex marveled at the length. He ran a paw down it and enjoyed the silkily smoothness. Her hair was like his fur. "Now I am convinced you have a Gatoan ancestor."

"You wish," she joked and closed her eyes.

So she liked to be petted too. That was good to know. He wanted to do more than pet her. His blood sang and he could feel his member coming alive. He would have her. His hunt was not over yet.

"Jewels!"

He scowled when he heard Jeremy's voice. Jewels jerked away, blushed pink and hurried around him and past his guards.

"Wait!" Dex yelled.

::I can't, my Prince. I must go. Jeremy does not bother me here unless he needs me.:: She paused and shyly added, *::Thank you. For the comfort.::*

And then his little human surprised him by giving him a mental kiss before breaking their connection.

He grinned. Happy at his progress with Jewels, he went back to walking the grounds. He missed his guards' expressions of worry. His mind was on his female and what he needed to do to win her for himself.

* * *

Larry Mellen sat in the shielded communications room and nervously waited for his conference with the President. He'd been ecstatic when he volunteered for and was accepted for this assignment. A chance to work with aliens was not something one passed up. It was turning out harder than he expected.

The Gatoans, especially Prince Dex, were volatile and unpredictable. The headstrong Prince wanted to take part in a psionic ceremony. Larry shook his head and bemoaned his eagerness to assume this post. The vid beeped, signaling an incoming call. Larry straightened and activated the screen. "Good afternoon, Mr. President."

"Liasion Mellen, I can spare five minutes. Please make this quick."

"Of course, Mr. President," Larry stammered before composing himself. "Sir, the Gatoans have requested to participate in the Choosing ceremony for Special Lt. Enbran."

The President's eyebrows rose and he stared. He didn't say a word. Larry started to sweat.

"How many?"

"Sir?" Larry stared at the President.

"How many do they want to place in the Choosing ceremony?"

Hearing the President's impatience, Larry stiffened. "As many as we will allow. The only stipulation was that Prince Dex be among the contenders."

"I will have a decision by tomorrow. Brigadier General Maussey has been singing your praises."

Larry preened at the compliment. "Thank you, Mr. President."

The President nodded and the screen went dark. Feeling more confident, Larry went to tell King Renten the news.

*   *   *

Renten had returned to the scout ship to speak with Master Chief Leftclaw about what he suspected was wrong with his heir. Dex's increasingly erratic behavior and fascination with the female could be one of two things. One meant death for the human. It was unheard of for a Gatoan to mate-bond outside their own kind, but that could be the other reason.

They entered the tiny meeting room and sipped their blood juice. Renten sagged into his chair, the weight of so many concerns pressing on him.

Leftclaw sat down. "The room is secured, sire."

"Thank you, old friend. I am afraid my son is experiencing heat."

Leftclaw sat up straight. "Truly? Which one?"

"I believe it to be the mating heat," Renten replied cautiously.

"This is great news, my King! We had despaired of it ever happening for him. This will definitely improve confidence in your bloodline."

"It is not that simple." Renten sighed at Leftclaw's puzzled expression. "I think the mate-bond will be to the human female that touched our minds when we first landed here."

Leftclaw surged to his feet. "Impossible! They are not like us!"

"No, you are wrong. They are very much like us. Perhaps this is why the bonding is trying to occur. The female does not seem adverse. She is baffled by her reactions to him, yet she is not rejecting them either. My son, on the other hand, does not realize what is happening to him."

"You must have a healer check him and verify the truth of the matter. If he will endanger this mission, he needs to go back to the ship."

"I know. He will fight me fang and claw. He might have to be collared." Renten ignored Leftclaw's horrified look. "I will not lose our new ally over my heir's lust. I have, however, decided to test my theory. The human female is losing her partner due to a peculiar problem with her psionic ability. The humans have a Choosing ceremony where telepaths of a certain age come and go through three trials. Those with the high scores are presented and then one is chosen as the female's new anchor. I asked, and permission was granted, for some of our males to be included. I, of course, told my son he could participate. He seemed thrilled at the news."

"But sire, what if he fails? Not having his mate-bond fulfilled will drive him mad."

"I am aware of the risk. I'm betting on my son. I just wanted you to be prepared, just in case."

"Yes, my King. Is there anything else?"

"Yes, please check on Rialla, I know she's probably feeling neglected. I want to wrap up negotiations and leave in four days."

"It will be as you order, my King."

Renten smiled. "Thank you, so much, old friend. Keep holding down the fort."

"Don't I always?" Leftclaw chuckled and watched Renten teleport off the ship. He stared out the window. Why would the prince react to one of the furless ones? Leftclaw had no answers, only more questions. He sighed and went to contact the main ship.

Chapter 18

Elenora bustled about the command center, but her mind was not on her work. Instead, she was rethinking the abruptness of thrusting a Choosing ceremony on Jewels. She had seen the younger woman's devastated expression and it tore at Elenora.

She would have done it differently if she could, but Jeremy was right. They couldn't wait any longer and, giving Jewels time to brood was never good. Elenora rubbed her neck, trying to relieve some of the tension from her body. Brigadier General Maussey was another area of concern. She disliked him immensely. His greed and need for revenge were unhealthy.

"Dr. Cosmit!"

She bit back a snarl. Even thinking of the irritating man was enough to summon him into reality. She schooled her features and turned to him. "Yes, Bg. General?"

"We've been summoned to a vid conference with the President. They want us there ASAP."

Elenora was surprised. She could tell that Maussey was too. "Yes, Sir." She swept by him and headed for the side room reserved for such conversations. She sat without waiting for Maussey to do so. She noted his scowl and felt a perverse joy at aggravating him.

He sat and activated the screen. The feed started and Elenora saw that the President was not alone. She shivered when she recognized his companion. She felt her stomach knot.

"Brigadier General Maussey. Doctor Cosmit. Allow me to introduce Colonel Manroe, an agent with the Psi-Ops division. He will be presiding over the Choosing ceremony."

"Sir, do we really need him? The Choosing has always been done without high-ranking officials present," Elenora objected. She did it, not for Jewels, but for herself and Jeremy. Manroe had a reputation that people whispered about. And if you were on his radar, nothing good ever came of it.

"Yes, Dr. Cosmit, we do. This is a special ceremony. We have aliens present who not only wish to watch, but have some of their warriors participate."

"What!" roared Maussey as he jumped to his feet, knocking his chair over. "No!" he slammed his fist down on the table. "I will not allow it! The ceremony should be for human psionics only."

"Sit down, Bg. General. You will allow what I order," the President sternly rebuked the man.

Elenora silently agreed with Maussey, but she wasn't going to foolishly yell at the President. "Sir, are you going to allow them to participate?"

It was Colonel Manroe who answered. "Yes, we are. In the rules for the Choosing, it states that 'a contender must have proven psionic abilities, be of good standing and of good health.' Nowhere does it say human psionics only."

She grimaced. She hated legal loopholes. "Sir, we should reconsider this plan. The last time such lasting contact was made

114

between Jewels' mind and a Gatoan's mind, she almost died. Do you wish to risk that again?"

"She will be fine," Colonel Manroe assured her.

"How do you know that? Are you her physician? No, I am. I'm telling you right now. The stress she has been under for the last week is debilitating to her performance as an officer. Sir, I must insist that the aliens be denied."

"Tell me, Dr. Cosmit, are you protesting because you really care or for appearance sake?" Manroe's penetrating gaze bore into hers.

Uncomfortable at his scrutiny, Elenora put her hands on her hips and glared. "Because I care. Why else would I object? She's fragile. I'm not going to let you break her to suit your own ends."

"It is unfortunate that you feel that way." The President leaned back in his chair. "Colonel Manroe is coming now to observe. The aliens have been told they will be participating, but we are limiting their entrants to three with the Prince being one of them. Now, if there are no further objections?"

Maussey opened his mouth to speak, but the President ignored him. "Good. I expect a live feed be sent to my office as well as Psi-Ops headquarters. We are all very interested in the outcome. We will adjourn. Good afternoon, BG. General, Doctor."

Elenora sat and fumed. She was so tired of the disrespect. After this Choosing, she was asking for reassignment. She didn't want to be Jewels' doctor anymore. And, Jeremy would be free to relocate with her. She stood, cast a sideways glance at the furious Maussey, and left him to his own devices. She had a Choosing to prep for.

Chapter 19

Dex impatiently watched the time counting down. He and his father had received word from Larry that the President had agreed to their admittance into the Choosing ceremony. He had let out a roar of happiness and felt like a cub all over again. This was the best news he'd had since coming to this world.

His father was less than pleased by his exuberant display of joy. Dex would not let that deter him. He flooded Larry with questions and listened intently as the Liaison explained how the Choosing worked. It was a three-day event and each day saw a different trial. Contenders were eliminated if they failed any portion of the tests. The top four would advance to Day Three and the final test. The contender who passed all tests with high scores and who had the best mental rapport with Jewels would be declared victor.

Dex thanked Larry for his help and turned to his father. "Whom will you choose for the other two slots?"

"Your two guards. Nipaw and Dipaw have earned the right."

He sized up his guards. They would be able to connect with Jewels, but he was more determined. "Very wise choices, Father. If you had decided on anyone else, it wouldn't be fair."

"Oh?"

"Nipaw and Dipaw scored in the top five of their class. No one else is alive from that top five. I know that these two are competitive with each other and now you're giving them a chance to best their Prince at something. All very good motivators." Dex stretched and yawned. "I'm going to rest up. Don't want to make a poor showing."

His father stared at him and Dex gave him an innocent look. "I will see you in three hours." He left the room, humming a melody that his mother had sung to him as a cub. Destiny had knocked and he was answering the call.

*   *   *

Colonel Manroe stood in the President's office and gazed out the window. "I think Bg. General Maussey was about to have a heart attack at the news of the Gatoans' participation. Would have saved us the trouble if he had died. One less pesky human to deal with."

"Chris, sometimes, you scare me," Dimitri retorted.

Manroe turned to look at the President and his best friend of twenty years. "I scare myself most times. But she won't be afraid of me," he muttered and tapped the window, his thoughts traveling along the web of possibilities. They were entering the critical stage where every word and action could collapse the plan and send them spiraling into destruction.

"Chris, do you regret any of the things we've done the last few years?"

"I don't know, Dimitri, maybe. If we hadn't, would the human race even exist? I know I play the "what if" game better than anyone alive, but that doesn't mean there are times when I wish I could choose

117

another way." He stopped speaking and closed his eyes. "Life is precious. I hate to lose even one."

"Maybe we shouldn't have read all those comics when we were kids. Then we wouldn't have such hero complexes," Dimitri quipped.

"Yeah, maybe. I'd better get going. They will be starting in thirty minutes. I like to arrive early and do my glower thing."

Dimitri chuckled. "Like I said, you scare me. I think you show scary better."

Chris opened his eyes and smiled. "That's what I'm paid for." He slipped his shades on. "Be ready to move on my signal. Things are going to go at a fast pace from here on out."

"I know." Dimitri left his desk and came to Chris' side. "Be safe, my friend." He clasped Chris' arm, who did the same with him.

"Destiny be our wings," they said together before moving apart.

Chris waved and teleported to his destination. He arrived outside the building and paused as his mind hit him with four possibilities. He grimaced and decided on the one to choose. He had to be alert. The web of chances was about to come alive and they were all going to have a bumpy ride.

*　　*　　*

Dex stood beside his father and barely kept from fidgeting. Doctor Cosmit was angry with them, but he didn't care. After two days of waiting, he had gotten his way. After the contest of skills was finished, he would claim his little human in all ways. He refused to leave her on this planet where she was abused and unappreciated.

::My son, be calm. You make the other contenders nervous.::

::They should be. None are worthy of her, Father. I will be all she needs.::

His father's tail smacked him across the back. Dex winced. *::What was that for?::*

::My son, did you speak with our royal healer?::

::No. I haven't had time.::

::Dex, my son, there was a reason. You will let him examine you after the first phase of this Choosing is over.::

Dex growled and froze when his father slammed a mental smack on him.

::That is an order, Dex!::

::Yes, my King,:: Dex ground out.

::Good. Now, behave, the little human approaches.::

Dex almost snarled at his father for using his name for the female. Sanity prevailed and he subsided. What was wrong with him? He ignored his father's concern and stared at the door. He watched Jeremy enter first. Dex had been secretly relieved to learn from the human male that he was not mate-bound to Jewels.

He and his father were shocked to learn that the Jewels was an incredibly powerful telepath, yet flawed. They had never heard of a person who couldn't create mental defenses to protect the mind. The humans had created an imperfect system to help her by using human males, called anchors, to shield her mind. It was only temporary and they had to exchange them every two years.

Dex grinned at Jeremy. The Colonel had done the impossible and lasted longer than any other anchor. Yet, even he was tiring. Dex felt sympathy for him. Protecting someone was an honor. To be told that you were failing would be a blow to the ego, even if it was anticipated.

He saw Jewels enter and sensed her agitation. He could smell her misery and pain. A surge of protectiveness hit him and Dex took a step forward to go to her. He found his way blocked by their guards.

"Move," Dex hissed.

"No, son. Remember the rules of our host or would you risk losing her? Patience," his father urged.

Dex's tail twitched and he struggled for control. Finally he found it. The guards relaxed and stepped aside. He saw that Jewels stood by Doctor Cosmit and the scowling Maussey. It seemed to be a normal reaction for the arrogant base commander. Dex didn't like the man standing that close to Jewels.

"May I have your attention please? The first phase will begin in five minutes. Follow Colonel Lingley and he will explain what to expect," Doctor Cosmit ordered.

"Go, my son. May you and ours bring honor to our people."

"I will, Father." Dex, flanked by the two guards, followed the humans into the other room.

Chapter 20

Once more, Fearnone checked his invis-shield. So far, none had detected him. Not even the Prince, who had sharper senses than most. It was comical that the Prince did not recognize the mate-bond heat raging in his royal veins. It was moments like this that brought Fearnone perverse joy. While others were awed and intimidated by royals, he knew them for what they truly were. Fallible, stupid, petty and mortal, the royals were driven by strong drives and desires like everyone else.

He had been on this miserable planet for almost a week, hoping for a chance to get close enough to assassinate Prince Dex. He never seemed able to get a clear shot at his target. And the female was proving to be even more elusive. He didn't know if it were by nature or just luck. No matter. He had a contract to fulfill. And besides, if he brought the Prince's head back on a plate, Queen Rialla had promised to take him as mate. It was an offer he couldn't refuse. So here he was, on the human planet, waiting, like always, to murder people.

Too bad he had to kill the female. She was young and her scent made his mouth water. Perhaps he would have fun with her first before killing her. He licked his lips at the thought. Yes, this job was giving him many perks. Quietly, Fearnone unpacked his weaponry and settled himself in the doorway of the building south of the training area. When Dex and the girl emerged, for he had no doubt the Prince would be victorious, Fearnone would be ready.

*   *   *

Maussey glared at Lt. Enbran, still furious at the unexpected turn of events. It was all her fault that he had to tolerate the interloping Gatoans. Now he had to find a way to sabotage the testing. And that doctor, Elenora, feigned outrage, but women like her thrived on chaos. She probably orchestrated this snag with Colonel Lingley.

"…Jewels, I'm sorry, but it's a Presidential order that the Gatoans be included."

"But, why? I mean, we know they are psionic, but we don't know the powers they wield. And, 'Hello', has everyone forgotten my encounter with their minds? I do believe a nosebleed and near-death experience count as endangerment."

For once Maussey agreed, but for different reasons. Once they let those walking carpets inside, everything would go downhill. He knew they would take over and enslave humans. He was not going to let it happen. Not on his watch.

"It does not matter, Lieutenant. This is by executive order. If you refuse, you will meet with the MDC again. And I assure you, Lieutenant, that they will change your mind."

Maussey grinned as he watched Doctor Cosmit chastise the young telepath. He prayed that the young woman would make a scene. If she was sent before the MDC, he had a few new punishments in mind and all involved her screaming in agony.

Jewels snarled, threw her hands up and stormed away. He was disappointed. He'd expected more of a fight. "Doctor, a word."

She came to him and waited. He thought of keeping her there for a while, but decided against it. The President and the UPO would be linking in to watch the Choosing.

"Doctor, I want her monitored 24/7. And I want all data sent to me first."

"Yes, BG. General."

Maussey wanted to laugh at her disgruntled expression. More work for Elenora, but she needed to remember who was in charge. "Dismissed." He headed for his seat as the vid-screens came alive.

"Sir, we have confirmed the sat-links to the UPO and the President are established. Feed is live and transmitting."

"Good. Inform the testers that we are ready to begin. Also, put Lt. Enbran's feed front and center." Maussey sat back and prepared to enjoy the show.

* * *

Jewels always hated this part. Psi-Ops called the event, "The Choosing," and she disliked the title. She really didn't get to choose. Her brain waves and Psi-Ops chose for her. She felt like an insect on a scanner, trapped and on display for all to see.

::Jewels, relax, please.::

::Easy for you to say, Colonel. You're not the one they'll take it out on if this experiment fails.:: She knew he didn't have a response to that

and they lapsed into uncomfortable silence. Jeremy hovered anxiously in her mind.

Elenora came over and touched her arm. "Time to start, Jewels."

"Okay, send in the first one." Jewels turned to her anchor. "Drop our shield."

Jeremy frowned. "Your mind, Jewels. It will..."

"...be unprotected, yes. That is part of the test, or have you forgotten your own Choosing trial? The candidate has to be able to shield my mind, Jeremy."

"I don't like it."

She smiled at his stubbornness. "You don't have to. Orders, remember? Now, drop it."

Jeremy reluctantly did so. Even though Jewels braced herself for the pain, it still caught her off-guard. She nearly fainted before forcing her body to calm down as the storm of thoughts assaulted her. "First one," she ordered, determined not to let the pain show.

A woman, shorter than herself with blond hair sat down. Jewels smiled tightly. She touched the woman's hand and frowned when the other girl jerked free. The urge to roll her eyes at the woman's behavior was tempting, but she ignored it.

Why they even allowed women in the testing aggravated Jewels. She'd never bonded with a female anchor. Too much pettiness and jealousy from the prospective women candidates interfered with any kind of joining. The majority of psionic men tended to be stunningly handsome, exuded sheer masculinity and often possessed charisma, power and money. All things females craved.

Finding a male psionic partner to bond with was harder still because the ratio of females to males was 10 to 1. The few women who made it every year into the candidate pool invariably got upset when put into a room with the men. They realized that they couldn't have any for mates on the off chance that one of the men might bond with Jewels. It created hard feelings. Jewels personally felt Psi-Ops should work to pair up psionics instead of wasting time sending females to her Choosing sessions.

"Thank you, Mina. You can go," Jeremy ordered.

The blonde shot Jewels a dirty look. ::*Watch yourself, slut. Not all of us like the fact you keep using and destroying our men.*::

Jewels gasped. Before she could reply, Jeremy was there by Mina, squeezing the girl's wrist hard. "If you ever spew thoughts like that again, you'll be mind wiped. Got it?"

Mina paled and Jewels gaped at Jeremy.

"Move!" He pushed Mina toward the exit.

Jewels stood up. "Jeremy!" She jumped when Mina slammed the door.

"Don't start, Jewels! It's people like that who give psionics a bad name." He turned to the observation window. "Doc, eliminate all female candidates from the list and send them home."

"Jeremy," Jewels tried again. When he ignored her, she walked over to him and touched his arm. She yelped when the emotions raging inside him flooded her mind. She couldn't pull away. She hadn't known her anchor felt that way about her. Her tears fell as she experienced his grief, anger, helplessness, and determination.

"I'm sorry," she whispered.

She found herself enveloped in his arms and he squeezed her too tightly. It didn't matter. He was her anchor, her safety. ::*Jeremy, you consider me family! I'm honored. I haven't had any in a long time.*::

::*Jewels, you're the little sister I never had. I refuse to let you be hurt. Besides, you don't swing that way. That's why Mina was really angry.*::

::*Oh!*:: Jewels blushed as the meaning of his words sunk in. ::*I didn't...um, wow!*::

Jeremy laughed and released her. "Okay, partner. Next victim."

She giggled. "Yes, I'm ready." And she would be, because the alternative was not an option.

Jeremy gave the signal and the next candidate entered.

*   *   *

Dex and his two guards watched the human prospects. He found it interesting when the three remaining females were removed from the room. He really wanted to release his claws and rip into the other males. They were not worthy of her. Only he was. Even his two guards were being allowed to vie for his female's attention.

One by one, the men were called until only Dex, his two guards and a black haired human remained.

"So, you are aliens."

He glared at the man. "We are," he growled and hoped the suddenly talkative human would take the hint to be quiet.

"Amazing. So, I guess, you read minds too? Oh, yeah, my name is Adam."

Must I suffer this fool, Dex thought sourly. "I am Dex. This is Dipaw and Nipaw."

"Weird names. Uh, different, I mean different," Adam amended when Dex's growl turned menacing.

"So, uh, did you see the girl? She's a looker. I heard rumors that being her anchor comes with perks, if you know what I mean." Adam leered and wiggled his hips suggestively.

Dex couldn't take it any longer. He bellowed his rage and ran at the human with his claws out. He was intent on gutting the stupid male for his insulting behavior.

Adam squealed and dove to the side, knocking over a table in his rush to get away from danger. Dex almost caught him, but was tackled by his guards.

::*My Prince, calm yourself! You will lose her if you don't stop!*:: Dipaw yelled in his mind.

Dex went limp in their grasp and fought his instincts. How dare that human speak of Jewels in such a manner! It was rude and demeaning. Maybe if the man lost his tongue, life would be better for everyone.

The door burst open and Jeremy, accompanied by several armed soldiers, rushed inside. "What is going on in here?"

"That, that alien tried to kill me!" Adam whined from his spot behind a table.

Dipaw and Nipaw helped Dex to his feet. He glared at the worm on the floor. Trust the wimp to cry foul. "I was not trying to kill him. Test his mettle, yes. But kill him, no. That would violate our treaty and make my Father angry."

Jeremy stared at Dex for a long moment. "I trust you three will be fine by yourselves if left alone?"

"Of course," Dex smoothly replied and grinned making sure that Adam saw his fangs.

Jeremy kept his expression stony and turned to Adam. "Very well. You, come with me. It is your turn."

Adam scrambled to his feet, scooted around the table and hurried out the door. Jeremy sighed and left with the soldiers.

"That was unpleasant," Nipaw remarked and sat in a chair.

Dipaw bowed to Dex and pulled out a chair. "Please, my Prince, sit. Your turn will be soon. And forget the silly human. The female is smart enough to see through his falseness."

Dex was disgruntled and frustrated. The urge to battle raged in his veins. He needed an outlet for his pent up emotions or else face turning feral. He slammed his paw down on the table, elongated his claws and dragged it, slowly, leave deep gouge marks on its surface. He ignored the concerned looks that Dipaw and Nipaw exchanged.

Soon, he and his little human would be one and nothing was going to stand in Dex's way.

Chapter 21

Master Chief Leftclaw strode purposefully toward the royal lair. He had promised to check on the Queen and he would do his duty. He really detested her, but Renten had chosen her and Leftclaw had to respect that choice.

He slowed his steps and perked up his ears. Leftclaw heard feminine laughter and the playful growl of a male Rieyad. His eyes narrowed and he unsheathed his claws. He stalked forward and froze in the doorway.

Queen Rialla sat nestled between the legs of King's Guardsman, Vin SenseAll, stroking his thigh and purring.

"You know, only a big, strong male can make me roar." She peered up into Vin's face. "I wonder if you can?"

"I believe I can, my Queen. No female should be neglected."

"I think so, too," Rialla simpered, her tail swishing back and forth.

"Let me prove it." Vin's paw slid seductively down her fur.

Leftclaw had seen enough. He let out a roar, startling the pair into scrambling apart. By the time they gained their feet, several guards had joined him. "Take that scum into custody and place the Queen in a comfortable confinement room. I will inform our King of these traitors."

Vin struggled, but the giant guards dwarfed him and held him fast.

Rialla sat on the floor and glared at Leftclaw. "How dare you?" she hissed. "I have needs."

"Which your mate should fill. As a royal, and as our Queen, you pledged yourself to our King, and him alone. No other male should take his place in your arms. You will be tried for your crime and punished accordingly. Take her away."

Rialla lunged at him and the closest guard easily captured her and walked away with the struggling Queen.

Leftclaw shook his head at this unexpected turn of events. He would wait until after the Prince's trials to inform the King of his wife's infidelity. Unhappily, he left the royal lair and headed for the war room. He needed to check on the progress of their enemies.

He arrived and found the place in an uproar. Leftclaw waited to see if anyone noticed his presence. When none of his warriors paid attention to his entrance, he grinned. It was time to remind them that awareness of their surroundings was paramount to survival. Leftclaw straightened and bellowed, "What is going on here? You shame me by your lack of skill!"

Every warrior in the room froze and turned with identical expressions of disbelief. Hastily they dropped to one knee in submission. "Master Chief!"

Leftclaw walked over to the Vasdji, Si Genhi. "Well?"

"Master Chief, we were about to contact you. Our three ships on the outer edges of this galaxy have reported that a fleet of Lupine ships are on there way here."

Leftclaw cursed. "How many?"

"Ten Sir, all dreadnought class."

"We cannot hope to battle them. This is bad timing all around. I must return to Earth to inform our king and ask the humans for help. Keep me updated every hour. Even if nothing happens, I want to know. Si Genhi, you are my second-in-command. Make sure you keep everything at the ready. Notify all warriors to be on standby."

"Yes, Master Chief Leftclaw. For our King and our pride!" Si Genhi bowed. His words were echoed by the others in the room.

Leftclaw nodded and left. Time was running out. They had wanted to hide the secret of their enemy and now they had no choice. They had to tell the humans. He only hoped they would be forgiving of the omission.

*   *   *

Jewels shook with exhaustion. The man called Adam sat before her. She looked in his eyes and shivered. She didn't like what she saw there. It made her want to hide. Jeremy shifted behind her.

::Jewels? What's wrong? Should we stop?::

::No, we can't. I, I'm just tired. We have the three Gatoans after this. I can't stop. Psi-Ops won't allow it. Please, lower the shield.::

::Jewels, just say the word, and I don't care what happens, I will stop this.::

::I know. It'll be okay. I'm ready.::

She felt Jeremy's concern and then the shield was dropped. She was reaching the end of her endurance levels. Only a little more and she could rest. Her mind was mostly numb to the pain from the constant barrage of thoughts.

"Hello, Adam. If you would please, attempt a shield."

"Of course." Adam smiled and Jewels felt a twinge of misgiving. He continued to smile and then she felt his mental touch. It was heat, it was smooth, it was...not the one she wanted!

"No!" she jumped to her feet and her chair fell to the floor with a crash. "Get out! Leave me alone!" Jewels clutched at her head and stumbled backward toward Jeremy who was beside her. His hand touched her shoulder and she screamed as the two men fought to shield her mind.

"Release your shield! The test is over for you." Jeremy ordered coldly and glared at the smiling younger man.

Adam glanced at her and she turned away and buried her face against Jeremy's chest.

"Now!" Jeremy thundered.

"Okay, okay. Sheesh, you people are an angry bunch," Adam grumped.

Jewels felt Adam's shield vanish and the familiar warmth of Jeremy's shielding settled over her mind. ::*Get him away from me!*::

::*Gladly!*:: Jeremy snarled.

Adam was hauled to his feet and dragged away still grinning.

::*Jeremy, don't let him come back. There's something wrong with him. Trust me, he's not what we're looking for.*::

::*Don't worry. I didn't like his smile anyway.*::

Jewels gave a weak laugh. "Let's finish this, please. I need to rest."

"Bring in the next candidate," Jeremy told the solider. He righted the chair and helped Jewels sit.

The door opened and one of the Gatoans glided in. Jewels noted that he kept his eyes on her. She shivered. The Onugra's intensity reminded her somewhat of Dex when his attention was completely on her. She collected her thoughts and gestured for the tall male to sit.

He seemed to melt into the seat. "I am Dipaw," he announced before she could ask his name.

"Thank you. I am Jewels. What we are doing is testing to see if you can shield my mind. My partner will lower the one he has around me and you must take over and provide shielding."

"I understand. I am ready."

Jewels smiled in relief. Finally a candidate who wasn't acting the fool. She nodded to Jeremy. She felt his shield drop and the barrage of thoughts hit her. She sucked in a breath and felt sweat run down her neck. "Proceed," she ground out.

Dipaw inclined his head and she felt coolness first, then warmth and then silence. "Oh! Thank you, Dipaw."

"You are welcome, my lady."

"Please, release your shield. We are finished for the moment." Jewels wondered why the Onugra's mental touch hadn't caused pain. She would think about it later. She felt his mind disconnect from hers and Jeremy's shield slid into place. "Dipaw, can you please send in whoever is next?"

"Yes, my lady." He rose and quietly left.

A few seconds later and a second Onugra appeared. "Greetings. I am Nipaw."

Jewels blinked. "Are you two twins?"

"Yes, my lady. We are. My brother was smiling so I take it everything went well?"

"He did just fine. Now it is your turn. Please sit. Colonel Lingley will drop his telepathic shield and it will be your job to replace his with yours to protect my mind. Are you ready?"

"Always," Nipaw grinned and settled himself in the chair.

They repeated the test, and, again, Jewels was surprised that there was no pain. She gratefully thanked Nipaw for his time and called for the next candidate to be brought out.

Her heart began to pound and, for one moment, she thought she caught a whiff of cinnamon and cocoa. She shook her head and sternly ordered herself to focus.

The door opened and Jewels knew who was coming even before he entered. The Prince had arrived.

Chapter 22

Elenora fumed while watching the trial. She cast a worried gaze at the screen with Jewels' vitals. The telepath wasn't going to last much longer at this rate. Elenora's objections had been overruled by Colonel Manroe, who lounged in a nearby chair. They didn't care about Jewels' health. She was a guinea pig to them. They liked to toy with her, push her to the point of breaking and then punish Jewels if she tried to fight back. It was sick and twisted and Elenora hated being a part of that vicious cycle.

"She's remarkable, isn't she?"

Elenora tensed. Manroe made her skin crawl. Dressed all in black, he wore a bored expression. It was his eyes, though, that were creepy. Solid silver, they made people mistakenly believe he was blind. Elenora knew, he saw more clearly thanks to his psionic ability and his education as a Parapsychologist.

"Yes, but she is human too. I thought the goal was to give her the best. So far this batch of telepaths has had the lousiest showing of any group. Excluding the Gatoans, who passed."

Manroe chuckled. "It appears that way, yes. We have our reasons."

Elenora shuddered. It was times like this that she was glad she was not psionic.

"Relax, Doctor. You don't want to scare our guests." He pointedly looked at King Renten and his two guards.

She studied them for any signs of stress. King Renten seemed very composed. Was he that confident of his son's chances? She frowned. She whirled around when an alarm sounded. Jewels' stress level and heart rate were increasing. Elenora glanced out the the window and sighed. The Prince's turn had come.

* * *

Dex ran through the open doorway when his turn came. He needed to make sure Jewels was all right. He needed to touch her mind and soothe her pain. He understood what the trial was about. And he cared. He wasn't so sure about the motivations of his competitors. You did not win a female by brute force. You had to fan her desires and win her heart. And, he planned to do just that.

He smelled her, that beautiful honey scent that was hers...and fear. The fear angered him. Who had made his little human afraid? He bared his fangs and stalked into the room. He noticed Jeremy moving in to a defensive position in front of Jewels. Dex sought calm. He did not want to frighten her.

"I'm not going to hurt her, Human. I'm sorry. I was reacting to the emotions in the room." He wouldn't have admitted his lack of control, but he wanted her to understand.

And she did. He saw a timid smile and the sweet aroma of her arousal filled his nose.

"I am ready to try your test," Dex murmured.

Jeremy looked at him and then Jewels. Dex felt their telepathic communication as a low hum along his mind. He wondered if the humans knew that they were loud. He would ask Jewels later. First, he had to win her trust. She gestured to the seat across from hers and he sat. His eyes never left her face.

"Jeremy, drop it."

Dex saw her flinch and immediately his mind sought hers. With a gentleness he didn't know he possessed, he touched her mind. ::*Little human, let me ease your suffering.*::

She was surprised. He filed that information away for later consideration. ::*Please?*::

::*I...yes...make it stop.*::

::*For you, anything, little human.*:: Dex blanketed her mind with his, shutting out all thoughts except for his and hers.

::*Thank you.*::

::*You are tired.*:: He stared up at the observation window and glowered. ::*You need to stop.*::

Her laugh touched his heart. ::*You sound like Jeremy. Always fussing at me to take it a little easier. That is something you have to learn about us, Dex. Psionics here are treated like outcasts or tools to be used by the highest bidder. And we are feared. If you make it and become my anchor, that is one of the things we would face as partners. Are you sure you want to do that?*::

::*I am always ready for a battle. I am a warrior and a defender. I will protect you and still let you be your own person. Your human leaders are foolish to harm such treasures.*::

::*We might do well together.*:: Jewels hesitated. ::*Can I ask you a question?::*

::You may.:: He twitched an ear and focused on her. He knew this moment would help or hurt his chance with her.

::Am I a tool to you and your kind?::

Dex sucked in a breath. Of all the things she could have asked, that was not one he had considered. Jewels was seeking trust and he wasn't sure how to answer. Was she just a tool? Not to him certainly, but would she believe that when they told her why they had come?

He opted for truth. *::Not to me.::*

::I see. Thank you for your honesty. The test is now over. You may drop your shield.::

He bristled. She hadn't liked his answer, Dex could see it in her eyes. *::What if I said no, little human?::*

::You wouldn't dare!::

Her incredulous look made him feel dangerous. *::I might, if you continue to tempt me.::*

::I'm not tempting anyone. You are imagining things!:: she snapped.

::Am I?:: He leaned back in his chair and regarded her flushed cheeks. Such a becoming shade of pink splashed across olive skin and the fire of indignation raging in her pretty violet eyes. Dex grinned. The hunt for this one was growing sweeter by the minute.

::Stop staring at me like that!::

::Like what?:: He taunted. She struggled not to squirm and he took note. Her arousal scent sharpened and he resisted purring his pleasure.

::Like you're going to eat me in a way that I wouldn't mind,::

Jewels whispered.

::Only if you wish it, my little human. I think though, for now, we must wait. Your friends are getting upset.::

::What?::

Dex smiled at her confusion. She had been so focused on him, she had forgotten the testing, he thought smugly.

"I am dropping my shield now, Jeremy," he informed the other male. *::Little human, until the next round.::* He wasn't surprised that she didn't respond. He knew desire and he knew what it felt like to fight against it. Dex was content with the knowledge that he had stirred hers in such a manner. Reluctantly, he released Jewels' mind. He stood, bowed, and quietly left the room.

Chapter 23

In the observation center, Colonel Manroe sat and enjoyed all the chaos this particular Choosing was causing. Psi-Ops had kept a close eye on the nineteen-year-old Jewels Enbran as she grew from a frightened four-year-old to a mature officer in the World Military. He, in particular, was intrigued by the abilities she used and those she had no knowledge of yet. She truly was a product of the Psi-Ops breeding program and a great testimony to what military discipline could do for one's life and career.

Manroe had always maintained that superiority of the species lay with psionics. And now his theory was bearing fruit. His superiors were shocked by the information that the Prince had an interest in Jewels. He, however, was not.

Even the meaning of her name was appropriate. She was like a precious stone, waiting to be molded, shaped and used to attract only the best the universe had to offer. Right now, three unified business corporations were fiercely bidding on Jewels' contract. Each of them wanted the telepath's skills. Psi-Ops hoped to cash in and make a tremendous amount of money. Not that the lucrative military contract Jewels was currently under was shabby, but the Psi-Ops Council wanted to branch out. They also didn't want their prized telepath to die at the hands of abusers like Maussey.

Manroe did wonder, though, if the Gatoan Prince would remain on

Earth if Dex did ultimately become Jewels' anchor. It was the one thing Psi-Ops had not considered. And, if the tension and simmering passion in the testing room was any indication, they might have a problem if the big cat wanted to take Jewels with him instead. It was not his job to worry about such things. He was here as an observer and information gatherer.

Several officers were under suspicion by the World Military High Command and, if the charges proved true, heads would roll. It was one of the tasks that he did enjoy. Cleaning house and taking out the trash was always a pleasure.

Dr. Cosmit called a break and the medical staff left to check on the applicants. She was still angry at him and Psi-Ops for the change made to the Choosing trials. Too bad. She was having to deal with it, just like Jewels and Jeremy were coping.

Manroe stretched and stood up. "Doctor, make sure Jewels gets the restorative drink and a fifteen-minute nap. Psi-Ops wants all three phases done by midnight. I know, Dr. Cosmit, that this is normally done over a 3-day period, but we don't have that luxury. I shall return at the start of the next phase. By all means, relax after I leave," he quipped and headed for the door. He had to make his report, but first he wanted to talk to Jewels.

The soldiers stepped aside and he went out into the hall. The white and tan walls were such stark and boring colors. Then again, the military was not supposed to be a place of warmth. He reached out with his mind and brushed against Colonel Lingley's shield. He chuckled when the shield tightened and he lost the trace. No matter. He knew where Lingley had taken her to rest. It took him a few minutes to get there. Manroe didn't knock. He walked right in.

Jeremy stepped into his path, blocking him from coming any closer.

"Down, Lingley. Bristling at me gets you nowhere. Now, where is the lady of the hour?" He saw the other man's hand clench, and then Jeremy pointed to a dimly lit portion of the room.

"Ah!" Eagerly, Manroe brushed by the anchor and went to Jewels' side. He pulled up a chair next to the cot. Her eyes were closed, but he knew she was awake.

"I must say, dear, that I was impressed by your showing. You did well. Psi-Ops is hopeful about this venture with the aliens. What I want to know is which candidate caught your eye? Don't bother feigning sleep. I know you're awake."

She muttered a curse under her breath and opened her eyes. "You were there, you should know."

"Jewels!" Jeremy hurried toward them, faltered and froze. Astonishment swiftly followed by rage crossed Jeremy's face. "What the...! Release me, Manroe!"

Manroe kept his gaze trained on Jewels as she slowly sat up and pushed aside the sheet. He read the fury in her posture. Excited by the thought of pitting himself against her, he used his telekinesis to choke Jeremy.

"Stop it!" Jewels demanded and swung her legs over the side of the bed. "I said, stop it!"

"Make me, little girl," Manroe sneered.

"Wrong answer," she hissed.

Manroe felt her anger erupt and braced himself by erecting a telekinetic shield. The shield was no match for Jewels' rage as she lashed out with her kinetic energy. He was flung clear of his chair and slammed into the wall far from the partners. The air whooshed out of his lungs and he slid to the floor, slightly dazed. He laughed maniacally as Jewels surged to her feet, her hair billowing about her head. He saw the tellatale sparks of her electrokinesis charging up.

He still had his telekinetic grip on her anchor. Manroe cleared his throat. "If you zap me, I'll kill him."

Jewels froze, indecisive, as her gaze swung from him to Jeremy and back again. "Let...him...go," she demanded, her entire body stiff.

Manroe hissed as his body protested his movements. He was going to be sore for days, but it was worth it to see her let loose. "No, I think not. I could kill him before you ever hit me with your power."

"Why? Why are you doing this? Isn't this Choosing bad enough? What do you want from me?" Her fists clenched and her electrokinesis fizzled out.

Her gaze slid to her anchor and Manroe saw the anguish. She might be hurting, but he had a lesson to impart. "Good girl, wouldn't want me to kill him by accident. I am doing this for one reason and only one. Psi-Ops is your family. Your family has need of you. Your weakness makes you a liability. You need to function without your anchor. But you can't. You're overly concerned for his welfare and have made yourself vulnerable as long as you worry about his life."

"Oh, geez, tell me something I don't know! You know you are a freaking bastard!" she snarled.

Manroe let go of Jeremy who staggered and gasped for air. He saw the murderous glare of his captive and knew one day Colonel Jeremy Lingley and he would revisit this moment. But not today.

"Let me educate you, Jewels Enbran. You were made by Psi-Ops to serve a greater purpose. That time is at hand. Whether you wish it or not, you will become Earth's only salvation." He stood and brushed his clothes off. "Well, I said my piece. Sleep well. You have ten minutes before Phase Two begins."

Jewels glared with hate as she crossed her arms and said nothing.

Manroe chuckled. Her spirit was good. Jewels would really need it if things played out according to plan. He whistled as he left the pair to think about his words.

Chapter 24

Adam sat with the other candidates but he remained aloof of their friendly chatter. He was close to his goal and if he played his cards right, the Gatoan Prince would fall into his trap. He smiled at the giant cat and all conversation ground to a halt.

Adam knew antagonizing the giant cat was a risk. He raised his head and threw a challenging look at the Prince. He saw the gleam of acceptance in the Gatoan's eyes as the Prince changed course and headed in his direction.

"You!" Dex roared and charged, his razor sharp claws out and ready to be used.

"Come to me," Adam whispered and when the enraged Gatoan was a few feet away, Adam used his kinetic shield. He grinned and then stared in horror as the Prince charged through it.

"Not possible!" he squealed and ducked the claws aimed at his head. He heard the other men scrambling out of the way. He was on his own. He yelped and dodged another swipe of Dex's claws. He was tiring, but the giant cat didn't seem to be. Adam ran, tripped and crashed to the floor.

He saw the Prince leap and he shut his eyes. After a moment, he peeked and found the angry Gatoan restrained by his guards. He grinned and stood up. "I'm going to file a complaint."

"No, you're not."

Adam whirled and saw Brigadier General Maussey in the doorway. "I'm not?"

"No, because you provoked the fight. If you wish to stay, I suggest you behave. And as for you," Maussey pointed a finger in the Gatoan's direction. "One more incident, treaty or no treaty, you're out of here."

"Understood," Dex growled.

"Good. The Lieutenant has rested and the second phase starts now. Remember, Gentlemen, the next person to cause a disruption and mess with my schedule will have their head handed to them on a platter." Maussey pointed at Dipaw. "You, come with me. You're up."

Adam sighed. Getting rid of the Gatoan Prince was turning out to be harder than anticipated. It was time to go to Plan B.

*　*　*

Lastbite paced the bridge of his dreadnought. His ship, along with the other nine in his fleet, had used the galactic gates to get to the Milky Way Galaxy in hours instead of days. That stupid cur, Bonebreaker, was harassing him with constant demands for updates. His Alpha would drive him mad before he even reached his destination.

"Beta Lastbite, our sensors have detected three Gatoan Explorer Class ships around Saturn. Your orders?"

He considered what to do. Engage the Gatoans or continue? The Gatoans couldn't hope to take on the dreadnoughts he had brought.

"They are no threat. Our mission is Earth and the human female. If they attempt to intercept, destroy them."

"Yes, Beta Lastbite."

"Beta, Sir, it is Alpha Bonebreaker."

Wearily Lastbite rubbed his eyes and cursed the gods for such an impatient Alpha. "Put him on the center screen."

Bonebreaker's image filled the view. All around the bridge, wolves whimpered and dropped their heads in submission. Lastbite barely lowered his. "My Alpha. What can I do for you?"

"How close are you to the planet?"

"We will be there in six hours. It will be nighttime and easier for us to grab the female."

"Excellent. Make sure you do not fail me, Lastbite. There are always others to take your place."

"Yes, my Alpha." Lastbite waited until the screen went dark before letting out an angry howl. He would cut his strings, soon enough. For now, he had to get that girl. Their contact on Earth had better deliver the female or death would be the least of the spy's worries. And Lastbite would be damned before he'd allow himself to be at his Alpha's mercy if things went wrong.

* * *

Elenora was disgruntled with the tests. Jewels and Jeremy looked ready to drop, but Maussey and that callous Colonel Manroe didn't care. At the moment, both men stood beside her as they stared in awe at the readings between Jewels and the Onugra Nipaw.

"It's amazing isn't it? Look how close their sync lines are lining up. It's a near perfect match!" Manroe crowed.

"Doctor, you said these readings only happen with the Gatoans?" Maussey demanded.

"Yes. The best readings come from the Prince and Jewels. I know that's not what you wanted to hear, but those are the facts. None of the human telepaths have even come close to matching her wavelengths."

"Which human has the closest sync factor?"

Elenora grimaced. "Adam does, but he won't be the final choice."

"Oh? And why is that?" Maussey snapped.

"He keeps trying to dominate Jewels. The pairing will never work if he's trying to control her. She is the one in charge. The anchor is actually a support position."

"That's absurd. She's not been alive long enough to be in charge. And, she's young and makes mistakes. The older person in the pair should be in charge, not some brat," Maussey argued.

Elenora shrugged. "Look, I don't make the rules or decide how it works. I just monitor the pair's health and mental synchronization. That's it."

Maussey grew thoughtful. Manroe grinned and went back to staring at the readings.

Elenora wished the Choosing was over before permanent damage was done to Jeremy.

Chapter 25

"Thank you, my lady." Nipaw bowed low and left the room.

Jewels and Jeremy didn't speak. Both of them were too tired to do anything except sit and try to breathe. Jewels was beyond exhausted. Never had the three trials of a Choosing been done in one day.

The only response to her pleas to stop was a lecture from the hateful Maussey and more restorative drinks ordered by Colonel Manroe to keep her energy up. If she had to down another one she would vomit.

Jeremy was in bad shape, too. Each trial was designed to be more demanding than the previous one. The only good news was that the original group of thirty was down to fourteen for the second round. All three Gatoans were still in the running. She wasn't surprised.

::Jewels, you okay?::

::This is insane, Jeremy! Are they trying to kill me?:: she wailed.

::I don't know. Can you feel it? There's a sense of urgency. I'm not sure why. I'm here and will stay by your side. No matter the outcome::

::Thanks. I needed that. Dex is next.::

::You like him, don't you?::

::Jeremy! I...,::

::You're blushing, Jewels. In fact, you're cheeks are really pink.::

::Stop it! You're embarrassing me!::

::Admit it, Kid. You got a thing for the giant furball.::

149

::He is not a furball!:: She huffed. *::He is strong and kind. And scary and handsome and...::*

::...And you'd jump in bed with him at a moment's notice,:: Jeremy teased.

::Maybe. I don't know. They are like us. I mean, he's got fur and his features are more feline, but he has a nose, mouth, eyes...and other parts,:: She stammered and looked at her feet.

::You are too cute when you act like this. Keep being bashful. The big guy likes that.::

::Oh, hush. Here he comes!::

Jewels perked up in her seat and smiled when Dex came in the room. That familiar tension gripped her.

In Dex's eyes, she saw a promise of something sensual she longed for. In that instant, Jewels made up her mind. She knew that he would be her anchor. She needed him to be her anchor like she needed air to live. The others could take a flying leap off a short pier for all she cared.

Elenora cleared her throat and Jewels guiltily looked over at the doctor. She'd forgotten the woman was in the room.

"Dex, this trial is to test mental compatibility. You have to be able to react to Jewels' emotions and help her remain stable and focused. This is imperative in the field. We are attaching sensors to monitor your brain activity as you do this exercise."

"Jewels, are you ready?"

"Yes, Doctor." Jewels cleared her mind. This phase of the Choosing was painful. Images would be relayed to her mind to evoke different responses. It was up to the candidate to help her make sense of the situation and act accordingly. There were thousands of scenarios and she never got the same one twice. It kept her and her potential partner on their toes.

"Okay, hit me." She closed her eyes and whimpered as the sensory implant took over and she fell into a nightmare....

Dex saw Jewels' body convulse and he moved to run to her side, but was restrained.

"No, Dex, you have to do this telepathically. Otherwise, you fail the test," Elenora explained sternly.

He growled and was impressed when the doctor didn't back down.

"Fine!" He focused on Jewels' mind and slipped inside. His body went limp as the sensor readings began to spike.

* * *

Dex stared about, trying to make sense of what he was seeing. It was a moment before he realized he was in some constructed mental hell. It all felt real. There were bodies, movement, and noises that hurt his ears.

"Jewels!"

He pushed people out of his way and more appeared. He paused and considered the situation. He was going about this the wrong way. He centered himself and reached for her...and then...connection!

Dex yowled his battle cry and dropped to all fours. He plowed through the crowd and into the street. He could smell Jewels' fear. "I'm

151

coming, little human!"

He turned left and skidded to a halt in front of a blue building with no windows. He unsheathed his claws and charged inside. Disbelief froze him as he took in the scene before him.

Jewels was bound by the wrists and dangled a few feet off the floor. Her face was battered and bleeding. A brutish male screamed in her face and punched her in the gut, knocking the air out of her.

Dex roared his fury and plowed into the man, sending them both rolling. He viciously clawed the man, not giving his opponent a chance to land a blow. With a final swipe, he cut the man's head off.

"No one hurts her. No one!" Dex snarled.

He padded over to Jewels and, using his claws, cut the rope that bound her. She was light in his arms and so still. He put his nose near her face and sniffed carefully. "Little human, my brave little warrior, I'm sorry I was late. I need to see those violet eyes. Let me know you are all right." He waited and when she didn't rouse, he gently began to clean her face with his tongue.

Jewels stirred and gave a hurt cough. Dex sighed in relief.

"You scared me, little human. But I will always protect you."

"You are silly," she whispered and opened her eyes. Jewels raised her trembling hands to his face and cupped it gently. "You came. The pain is gone when you're here. Why are you different? What is this between me and you?"

"I don't know, little human. I must do something now. I will be gentle. If you will permit me, that is."

"I trust you."

He saw the truth in her eyes. Dex lowered his head and kissed her. It was everything and more when his lips touched hers. He was drowning in his first taste of her. Honey, just like her smell. Jewels was eager, her hands tangling in his fur as she deepened the kiss. He growled his frustration. It was nice to do this, but he wanted the real thing. Her skin against his fur. His mouth exploring her body. Her mind locked with his.

When her mind latched on to his, something clicked in place between them. He didn't stop to analyze it. He only knew that he felt a sense of completion that had been lacking before.

Reluctantly he ended the kiss and Jewels mewled a protest. Her lips were swollen and she stared heatedly at him.

"Little human, we must stop. You must wake up. I promise, I will finish what we started here."

"Okay, I'm going to hold you to that," she whispered.

Dex laughed. "I'm counting on it. Now, wake. We have something to complete in the real world."

"Oh, joy," Jewels muttered and closed her eyes.

He watched her dream self vanish, but the bond between them was solid. He would always be near to help her. Dex willed himself awake.

Chapter 26

King Renten sat up straight in his chair and his two guards turned to him with wide astonished eyes.

::Our Prince has found his mate!:: The cry echoed along the mental pathways shared by the royal guards and the royal family.

Renten grinned. His son had done it! Only one test remained before the humans would recognize what Renten had already known would happen. A new pairing and hope for an even better future.

*   *   *

Master Chief Leftclaw was unhappy with the situation on the main ship. The crew was restless and gossip was rampant on the topic of the Queen's confinement. Added to the chaos was an approaching fleet of Lupine dreadnoughts. Things were going to be dicey soon and the people needed to see their monarch onboard and in charge.

He took the four warriors who remained with him and flew the scout ship back to the flagship. He would be more effective there.

"Si Genhi, report!"

"Master Chief, the Lupine fleet has slowed near Mars. They will be here near the end of the second phase of the human Choosing ceremony."

Leftclaw cursed the timing. "And our ships?"

"Not too far behind. At least a two hours gap."

Leftclaw stroked his chin. "Stay in observation orbit around Earth. If we need to fight, we will. Our King and Prince will be returning soon." He stared down every male on the bridge. "Now is the time to show we are warriors!" He let out a roar and was joined by the others.

"Contact our King on the wrist comm. It is time the humans see what technology we can offer them," Leftclaw ordered. He turned his attention back to the screen. Let the enemy come, they were ready.

*   *   *

Colonel Manroe yawned and checked his watch. He felt the mental call from Psi-Ops giving him the green light. He smirked. Everything was coming to pass. Only one phase left of the Choosing. Four contenders remained. Manroe wanted to offer Jewels encouragement, but he couldn't do anything more for her. He needed to get back to his post. He stood, stretched, and shared a knowing glance with King Renten.

::*We know your secret, Gatoan King.*::

::*I thought you might. You are the only human not perturbed by the events happening.* ::

::*True. Your enemies have come knocking at our door.*:: Manroe nodded when Renten stiffened. ::*In fact, your Master Chief has been trying to reach you. However, I couldn't allow that. But now,*:: Manroe released his telekinetic hold on Renten's communication device. It

155

gave a shrill ring, startling everyone else in the room.

Renten's eyes narrowed. ::*You tread a dangerous road, human psionic.*::

::*I know. It's why they call me Shadow. I know all and see all. I even see how this will end. It's no fun if I tell you, so I shall take my leave. Just remember, hope can only blossom when love and truth are given freely.*::

::*I hate it when farseers give messages. You're too cryptic.*:: Renten growled in annoyance.

::*True, but if we aren't cryptic, no one pays attention. Good luck to you.*:: Manroe saluted the Gatoan monarch and quit the room, ignoring the whispers and Maussey's demands to know where he was going.

*　*　*

Renten wasn't sure what to make of that psionic, Colonel Manroe. And he was mildly surprised to be paged by mechanical means rather than telepathic. "I need to speak to my ship. Is there some place private I can go?"

The Doctor pointed to a small office. "You can go in there and close the door. It's a shielded room," she added.

"Much thanks, Doctor Cosmit." Renten flanked by his Rieyad and Loprofir guards hurried to the room indicated. Renten closed the door, yanked up the faceplate on his wrist comm. "What?"

"My apologizes, your Majesty. We have a situation brewing up here. The enemy is knocking at the door. When will the Choosing end?" Leftclaw appeared a little flustered.

"Soon. I am sorry, old friend, that you couldn't reach me. It seems the psionics here are full of surprises. We will be there as soon as we can."

"Yes, my King. Keep safe."

Renten ended the call and stared at the door willing his son to claim the prize. He went back out to the main area to wait for the victor.

Chapter 27

At the UPO's North American headquarters, all hell had broken loose. Reports were pouring in from the the other HQ branches. Several "somethings" were approaching the planet and the military and scientific units were scrambling to uncover what it was.

Dimitri sat in his office with a grim look. He glanced at his advisors and friends. Each had a stake in this. "Well, Chris, guess I lose the betting pool on whether you were right or not."

Manroe snorted. "I keep telling you not to bet against my record. It's the only good thing about me."

"Got that right," Brion muttered.

"Don't start, Xavier, or I swear I'll teleport you into an active volcano," Chris growled.

"Children! Can we please focus? The Lupines are here. I have to go give a quick speech to the UPO and the World. We will continue this conversation when I get back. Until then, play nice," Dimitri warned and left the four men behind.

He strode with purpose into the general session room. His presence quieted the noise and all eyes turned to him as he took the podium.

"My friends, today is a day that we, at the Executive Office, thought would never occur. We have discovered not only new allies, but enemies as well. Our enemies, have been walking among us for a few decades, never directly harming us. They have infiltrated every part of our society. We have prepared for such a contingency. We urge you to follow the emergency plans that are being handed to you. We promise that our victory will be swift and decisive. That is all."

The room erupted in loud shouts for more answers, but Dimitri ignored them as he exited through a side door. Hinson, Zenath, Brion and Manroe waited for him in the small conference room. They all wore stern expressions and he grimaced.

"Well, that went as well as could be expected," he joked.

"True. Earth's people will forgive us in time for not informing them sooner, but we had too much riding on this. The new fleet is ready and waiting. We just need to get the girl on the lead ship. All military psionics are being flown to their respective ships even as we speak," Hinson informed him. He handed Dimitri a status pad.

He read it quickly. "And the Choosing? Are they on the third phase now?" He looked at Zenath.

"Yes, Sir. Your security double noted that the Gatoan Prince will most likely be the victor."

"And the readings between the pair?"

"Off the charts, just as I predicted. She's bound to him. She will fight to keep him alive and that in turn will save humankind," Manroe added smugly.

Brion cleared his throat. "Sir, one of the Lupine agents is posing as a candidate. He has plans to grab the girl and give her to the enemy."

"Keep a guard on her. We can't afford to lose our biggest asset. I think it would be better if they took the Prince. Nothing like a little motivation to work a woman's emotions up." Dimitri handed Hinson the status pad. "Come, my friends, we have a planet to save."

"I will catch up to you later. There is one more small matter I must take care," Manroe informed them before teleporting away.

"I swear that one day Chris' secrets are going to kill him," Zenath muttered.

Dimitri shook his head. "Let's go!"

"Yes, Mr. President."

Hinson led them outside where a shuttle waited to take them to the starship they would use. The small group climbed in and took off for the launch pad, knowing that time was swiftly running out.

*　*　*

Fearnone looked up at the sky. Night had come and the humans had yet to emerge. He was beginning to get that feeling that told him the job had gone bad. Perhaps he should abandon this endeavor. He shifted his stance and prepared to leave.

"You know, that wouldn't be a wise move, Furball."

Fearnone tensed and felt a weapon poked into his back. "How did you see me?"

"The invis-shield was invented here on Earth. We track where our merchandise goes. Now, up. Nice and easy. One wrong step and you'll be a pretty rug on my floor."

Fearnone stood. He hated not being able to see his captor's face. "Do I get the honor of knowing who you are?"

"The name's Manroe. Unfortunately, I can't let you stay here. I will take what you know and use it to help her."

"What do you mean?" Fearnone demanded.

"Oh, nothing much. Just this."

Those were the last words Fearnone heard before Manroe's hand plunged into the back of his skull and he began yowling in pain.

Chapter 28

Jeremy was beyond worry. They were taking another break but Jewels wasn't doing well. She was almost lifeless and that was not something he'd ever seen her be. It was frightening. He felt the tiredness and her pain. He tried to soothe her, but she waved him off. Jeremy knew what the problem was. During the second phase he had felt Dex and Jewels' minds entwine and bond. No matter what anyone else did, it was useless. The two were mated.

He knelt by the cot and touched her head. She was burning up. "Jewels, I'm going to get Dex."

She feverishly grabbed his hand. "No, the rules. Remember the rules."

"The rules can kiss my..."

"Jeremy! Please, I'm fine," Jewels insisted.

"No, you're not! You don't get it, Jewels, because it's never happened to you before. It's the bond heat. It only happens when you're with a psionic who completes you. You only get it once in a lifetime." He didn't hide the bitterness behind his words.

She interlocked her fingers with his, her eyes glazed with pain. "Tell me."

Jeremy snorted. Even though she was hurting in a big way, she still worried about him. It was humbling. She needed to hear his words so he told her his story.

"I was about your age and there was this girl. I fell for her, but she, she didn't want me. In fact, she ended up marrying my best friend. We were all psionics and I almost died because of her refusal of our bond heat. It took a lot of effort and some dedicated healers to save my life. I went into the military after that and here I am today."

"Jeremy, that's awful!" Jewels whispered.

"I don't need pity, I want you to understand. Knowing Psi-Ops, they didn't educate you about the matter. And you're suffering because of it. The only way to ease the heat is for you and Dex to be intimate. And no, I'm not talking just about a joining of the minds."

She clamped her mouth closed and shook her head. "I can't. What if he doesn't want me in a forever kind of way? What if I'm just a diversion?"

He smoothed her damp hair back from her forehead. "Trust me, you're not, Jewels. You're the kind of gal a man would willingly shackle himself to. And if he didn't think that way, then he's a fool."

Jewels giggled, grimaced and then moaned in pain. Jeremy looked at her and made a decision. He hadn't forgotten the rest of the orders he had been given when he and Jewels were first assigned this mission. He had been sworn to secrecy, but time was against them. He untangled their fingers and stepped away. "I'll be right back, Jewels."

She didn't answer for she had slid into a fitful sleep. He hurried to the waiting room and shooed the guards away. He opened the door and beckoned for Dex to come to him. When Dipaw and Nipaw moved to follow, he waved them back.

Jeremy waited until Dex joined him in the hall and closed the door.

163

"What is it, Human?" Dex demanded.

"Jewels needs you. You need her. I'm about to do something to help you both. It'll probably burn out my gift, but Jewels means that much to me."

Dex gave him an interested look. "Go on."

Jeremy grinned. "I have a talent that is classified above top secret. I was given authorization to use it at my discretion should the need arise. I figured this was what they meant."

"Who is 'they' that you speak of?" Dex frowned.

"Doesn't matter. Hold on to my shoulder. And whatever you do, don't let go."

"Understood."

Traveling back in time was harrowing and dangerous. Jeremy had to be completely one with his gift or risk losing himself in the streams of time. He concentrated on when he wanted to be. He felt the familiar burning in his mind and ignored it. It was always strange watching the surroundings blur into a swirl of colors before becoming normal again. He gasped and stumbled backward.

Dex steadied him and stared with wonder. "You humans continue to astound me. Even we do not possess this talent."

Jeremy gave a rueful laugh. "Yeah, well, I don't use it often. Go in there. Give her what she needs. I'll be back when you're done."

Dex extended his paw and Jeremy shook it. "You are a true friend, Jeremy Lingley."

Jeremy smiled and walked away.

Dex stared at the door and went in, anticipation humming in his veins. This was it and he couldn't wait to show Jewels how much she meant to him. He saw her on the bed, moving restlessly. Dex knew she was aware of him. Her mind called to his and he reached out blanketing hers with his shielding. He was buffeted by the raging heat of desire that consumed her mind and body.

He gasped and suddenly a lot of things made sense. His father's insistence that he see the royal healer, his extreme possessiveness of Jewels, and his own awakening desire meant only one thing. The mating bond had started between them. He had to sate it or go mad. Apparently, she was having the same problem as he. Dex was thrilled. He knew Jewels felt some lust toward him. He didn't want to settle for just lust. He wanted it all.

He stopped at the cot and knelt. He slowly pulled the thin sheet off her. She was scantily clad and he wondered if she normally slept without clothing. If she didn't, he would make sure she started.

::Hello, little human. Do you trust me?::

::Dex? I'm so sleepy and hot. What's wrong with me?::

::I need to quench your fire. Do you trust me to do that?::

::I trust you. Help me, please. I feel like I'm crawling out of my skin. I ache, Dex.::

::I know, my little human. Let us get you out of your clothing and we shall go from there.::

::Yes, please, it's hot in here.::

::Not as hot as it will be.:: He purred deep in his throat and unsheathed one claw.

Dex studied her clothing and decided the easiest way to remove it was to cut it down the center. He started with the one covering her breasts. It was no match for his claws. Her breasts were fuller, more round than the females of his kind, but he didn't mind. Hers were perfect and his. He buried his face in them and heard her gasp.

Her fingers wove their way into his fur and she tugged, none too gently, pulling his head closer. Dex snaked out his tongue and licked one nipple slowly, laving his tongue around it. She moaned and her hands ran restlessly down his fur.

::Do you like this, my human Onugra?::

::Yes, I didn't know it could be like this. I need you.:: She wriggled beneath him.

::Have you mated before? If not, I must go more slowly.::

::Yes, but only twice, and never worth remembering.::

::That is a shame. You should be pampered and cherished.:: His nose twitched and he happily filled it with her sweet honey arousal. He moved his mouth from her nipple and heard her protest.

::I will make you roar, my little human. First, I wish to savor every inch of you.:: He nuzzled and licked his way down her chest, to her belly, and laughed when his whiskers tickled her and she giggled.

Dex buried his nose right above the little scrap of cloth that covered her womanly core from his gaze. It was soaked with her juices. She was more than ready. Growling, he took it in his teeth and tore it from her body, leaving her bare. He repositioned himself between her thighs and looked at her. Her eyes were on him. She was ready and expectant.

::I will rage inside you, fill you and not stop until you scream your

heat to the heavens.::

::Will it hurt? Felines here have barbs on their...members. Are you the same?::

::We control ours, my Onugrass. We use them only when we wish to have young.:: Dex really wanted to sink into her depths, but he held still, waiting for her to choose.

::Please, take me! I want you to be one with me. Love me, Dex, love me.::

::Gladly, little human.:: He pulled the string that bound his loincloth around his hips. It dropped and he set it aside. His member sprang free, stiff and full of life for the first time since he came of age to be a male. This human female was giving him a special gift.

::For you, Jewels, my precious gem of life.:: He slid in to her slick, hot welcoming core and felt the tight grip around his shaft. He purred low, vibrating them both with the sound.

Her mind wrapped thoroughly with his. He began where she ended and she completed him. He set a slow, languorous pace that drove their inner fires higher to an all-consuming blaze. His fur glided along her body with his thrusts. She curled up and pulled his head down, kissing him as the new position sent him deeper. He was nearing climax as was she.

::Come fly with me. Ride the wave,:: Dex urged as he increased his pacing.

"Dex!" Jewels cried, tears of happiness running down her face, as she gasped and rocked her hips. Her head flung back, and she gripped his fur tightly. Her mewling, longing cries filled the room.

The pain from her tugging his fur was nice and he growled loudly. "Now, I mark you as mine." He thrust hard and his roar of triumph mingled with her scream as she came hard, her inner muscles clamped him, squeezing him and sending shudders of orgasmic waves through her. He felt his seed fill her and he shuddered with the ripples of pleasure that sang through his mind and body.

He wrapped his arms around her as their bodies tried to remember how to be separate beings. "My mate," Dex purred contentedly and licked her nose.

"Silly male," Jewels whispered, but her eyes shone with love. "What time is it?"

"Doesn't matter. This was our time. We are now mate-bonded. In your human speech, we are married."

"Married! What? Now wait just a second, Dex," Jewels started to protest and he kissed her silent.

"Shh, little human. I am yours, you are mine. I will be your shield and protector. There is no other. Now, I must leave you. Sleep and when you wake, we will do the final phase of this Choosing and leave this place."

"Dex, I just can't leave," she retorted, but her eyes were closing.

"Sleep," he ordered and forced her body to rest. He carefully slid from her, feeling for a moment bereft. He started licking the mating fluids off her. Dex even cleaned his whiskers, wanting to savor every drop of his mate. He would never get enough of her. Once he finished, he pulled the sheet up and covered her.

Dex put his loincloth on and kissed Jewels' forehead, a huge grin on his face. She was truly an Onugrass. He went out to the hallway and nodded to Jeremy. "Thank you."

"No problem. She deserved at least one moment of happiness."

Dex grew wary. "What do you mean by that?"

Jeremy shook his head. "Can't tell you. Laws of the universe and all that jazz. Remember that Jewels' love is a powerful thing." He clamped a hand on Dex's shoulder.

"But!" Dex didn't get to finish for the world spun and he lost consciousness.

Chapter 29

Jeremy felt bad about what he'd done to Dex, but orders were orders. This was one of the few times when he enjoyed having time manipulation abilities. He'd frozen time and now he had to hurry. He placed the unconscious Prince in the room with the remaining candidates. The deed was done. Jeremy marveled once again how still everyone looked when caught in a freeze.

He knew Jewels was resting, felt her contentment. Jeremy was glad to be able to give her this one gift. He looked at his watch. Time to let events play out. Jeremy left the holding area and went back out to the hallway. He strode down the corridor until he reached the room where Jewels slept.

"Time to wake, Sleeping Beauty." Jeremy closed his eyes and became one with time. He felt life resume and he let go with a gasp. His head throbbed and he ignored it as he slid his shielding over Jewels' mind.

::Hey, Kid, wake up. Time for the last phase.:: He entered and stood at the foot of the cot.

::Hmm? What? Is it now?:: Jewels rubbed at her eyes and sat up, her long hair falling forward to cover her breasts.

The look on her face was comical as she remembered what had transpired. And that she was nude. Jewels squeaked and jerked the sheet up around her chest. She blushed and he couldn't help teasing

170

her.

"Hey Kid, why you blushing?"

"I am not!" she snapped at him and ducked her head.

"More clothes are in the bureau. Get dressed. We have to be ready to go in five minutes."

She rolled her eyes and then pointed at the door. Jeremy laughed and left so she could put her clothes on.

Jewels emerged in under five and appeared healthier and happier than before. Jeremy smirked. Sometimes being a psionic was an awesome thing. They entered the training area where Dex, Nipaw, Adam and Dipaw stood.

The tension was noticeable, but Jeremy didn't give the four males time to think. "Gentlemen, this is the last phase. The winner will become Lt. Enbran's anchor and I will get a well deserved vacation," he joked, making sure to send Jewels mental reassurance that he didn't mean the words the way they sounded.

::I know you don't mean it that way, silly Anchor,:: she chided Jeremy.

Dex growled at his statement. Jeremy ignored him. "When you are called, you will be teleported to a different location. At that time, you and Jewels will be thrust into a scenario where you must act as anchor and as a fighting pair. You will not be released from the simulation until all opponents are eliminated. Adam, since you are the only remaining human candidate, you will go first."

Adam's overly enthusiastic expression annoyed Jeremy. He turned to his partner. "Jewels, you ready?"

"Yes," she answered, her voice flat as she shot Adam a hostile glare.

::Jewels! Play nice. You may not like him, but he had high psionic compatibility with your mind.::

::Yeah, well, you can take that compatibility and...::

::Don't go there, Jewels. Get going, that's an order.::

::Fine,:: she huffed and teleported herself and Adam from the room.

Dex moved forward. "What trickery is this? You did not say she could teleport!"

"You didn't ask. Besides, you three need to report to your King. Something has come up."

He snarled and lunged, but Jeremy wasn't there. He'd teleported and stood by the door.

"Not nice, Kitty Cat. The only way you can help her is to go to your father and prepare for battle. Your flea infested friends have arrived and are coming for Jewels. We need you fighting, just as she will be."

"You! She trusted you!" Dex accused.

"And I'm sure she'll let me know in no uncertain terms how betrayed she feels after we survive the ten dreadnoughts bearing down on us. Now move! We've got a planet to save." Jeremy opened the door and waited.

Dex's menacing glower would have cowed a lesser man, but Jeremy wasn't afraid. He knew the big guy would make the right choice. After another moment of posturing, he stomped by him with

172

Dipaw and Nipaw in tow.

Jeremy waited until they had left before sending out a telepathic call to Elenora to proceed with her part of the plan.

Chapter 30

The testing command center was in an uproar. Maussey's furious ranting filled the room. He had watched Jewels and Jeremy enter the training area where the three Gatoans and Adam waited. After a moment of talking, Jewels, along with Adam, had vanished.

The vid feed suddenly died and despite his yells to fix it, the feed never came back up. One by one the other views became static and the observation room was blind.

"Status report, now!" he bellowed at a frantic Private.

"Sir, we've been locked out of the system."

"No!" Maussey slammed his hand down on the table. He whirled and stalked toward Renten. "It's all your fault! You filthy beasts came here and ruined everything. You will pay for disrupting my plans!"

Renten's composed expression had Maussey seeing red. He jerked his gun from its holster and raised it to fire at the Gatoan King.

"I don't think so, Sir."

Maussey blinked, distracted by Dr. Cosmit who had stepped between him and the Gatoans. "I knew it! You are in on this plot! I will shoot through you, you conniving woman!"

"Sorry, Sir, but you won't. I'm afraid it's the end of the road for you."

"Meaning what, you stupid girl!"

"Oh, it's easy. You've been made. They know that you and a Lupine agent had plans to grab Jewels. UPO and Psi-Ops have had countermeasures in place for months. They also know about your money laundering and acceptance of bribes. This is a cleansing, BG. General Maussey, and you're about to become part of the trash."

"You arrogant bitch!" Maussey pulled the trigger and screamed in disbelief when electricity surged from the weapon into his body. He howled and and went to his knees. He couldn't make his finger release the trigger and the last thing Maussey saw as his eyes rolled up in his head and unconsciousness claimed him was Dr. Cosmit's smug grin.

"Whew, that was nasty," Elenora remarked when Maussey's body finally stopped twitching. She glanced at Renten and grinned at his amusement.

"You humans are very surprising. Ah, my son arrives."

Dex charged into the room, claws ready. "What happened?"

Elenora grinned, walked over to Maussey's body and nudged him with her shoe. "Just taking care of business. You guys need to get going. The Lupines are about to meet our mighty fleet and we thought you would like to be part of it."

"Remind me never to anger a female healer." Renten bowed to her and she smiled.

"Duly noted. And Dex, don't worry. Jewels will find you. She can't live without you."

Dex gasped, recovered his composure and went to his father's side.

"Good luck." Elenora waved, turned her back to them and started shouting orders at the staff.

Renten chuckled. "What a woman! Dex, teleport us now. Master

Chief Leftclaw is having a fit and the humans need some help."

"Yes, Father."

Renten felt the gentle pull of Dex's power as they returned to their flagship. Leftclaw stood, barking orders as the bridge crew rushed to comply.

"Status, Master Chief." Renten went to the captain's chair and sat, his tail swishing slowly.

"We're trying to find out which of Bonebreaker's Betas he sent so that we can better formulate our strategy. For whatever reason, they did not destroy the three ships we had monitoring this galaxy's borders. It will cost him."

"Yes it will, old friend. The humans apparently have a fleet of their own. Another thing left out in our full disclosure session. Unexpected, but welcome news. We must be ready to assist."

"My King, the ten Lupine dreadnoughts have stopped near Earth's moon."

"Dex, sound the alarm. Battle stations. We must protect our allies. For Felinia and for Earth!" Renten roared.

The bridge filled with a resounding cheer as the Gatoans readied for battle.

Chapter 31

Jeremy waited until the Gatoans had returned to their ship before joining Elenora in the testing command center. He smiled in satisfaction. He gestured for the two soldiers that accompanied him to remove the unconscious Maussey. "Put him in the transport outside. He has a date with a court martial."

Elenora laughed and Jeremy gave her a surprised look. "What's so funny?"

"Fate. Destiny. Whatever you'd like to call it. When they say what goes around, comes around, they meant it in his case. Stupid fool, just one charge alone will earn him a flogging like the one he gave Jewels. In this instance, justice works well."

Jeremy grinned. "I like the way you think. I'd love to stay and play, but I have a ship to catch. But first..." He dropped to one knee before Elenora, reached in his pocket and pulled out a ring. "Will you marry me?"

Her mouth fell open in surprise and Elenora stared him for a long moment before whispering, "Yes."

The room erupted in cheers and he slid the ring on her finger, stood, and kissed her long and hard. Jeremy stepped back with a smug grin. "I think a miracle occurred. You're speechless." He caressed her face. "I've got to go. I'll see you later."

"You be careful out there." She hugged him and stole one more kiss.

Jeremy didn't mind. He hoped that now Elenora understood what she meant to him. He moved from her arms, waved and teleported to the space launch pad.

He took a moment to get his bearings and then he was off at a brisk clip to the assembly room. Jeremy entered and chuckled at the loud mental greetings from the eleven psionics in the room. Four women and seven men came to their feet.

"Colonel Lingley, nice of you to join us," Manroe drawled.

"You know I'm always on time. And don't think I've forgotten the stunt you pulled earlier tonight. I'll settle with you later. Right now, Jewels needs us. Is the ship ready?

"Of course. You know how it is. A little bit of psionic power goes a long way. Now, let me introduce your crew, Colonel." Manroe walked over to the psionics and stopped at a petite black-haired woman. "We picked them all based on past experience with working with Jewels. She has known each of their minds or at least touched them so that they are not foreign to her. This is necessary for her adjustment process once we get her on the ship."

Jeremy nodded. "Makes sense. She always performs better if she's relaxed."

"This is Patrice, she's your linguist and cryptologist. She is highly skilled in both." Manroe smirked. "Her very talented mouth does occasionally get her in trouble."

"Hey, I can't help it that I'm good at foiling the bad guys' secret codes."

Jeremy grinned. He remembered Patrice from an op they did three years ago. It was one of the few times that he'd ever seen Jewels want to be in another woman's company.

Manroe rolled his eyes and continued with the introductions. "This is Robin, your science officer. Next to her is Yasmine, chief medical officer. Our last lady, but certainly not the least, is Melinda, your parapsychologist. Yasmine and Melinda are responsible for your overall physical and mental health, especially Jewels' stress and performance levels."

"Duly noted." Jeremy turned to the seven men. "Gentlemen." He realized that none of the gathered psionics had a higher rank than him, though several were older and had served in the military longer.

"Mike is on weapons. Nathan is your engineer. Tyler has communications. For your navigator we gave you the best, didn't we, Lionel?"

The portly older man stepped forward with a laugh. "You know I wouldn't pass up an opportunity to work with Psi Ops' famous Lt. Enbran. Besides, every living thing needs someone to give it good directions and I do that better than anyone alive."

"Too true." Manroe waved him back and faced the remaining three men. "Malcolm is in charge of security."

"Hello, Colonel," the giant black man grunted.

Jeremy remembered Malcolm. He was a man of little words, but the big guy could take down an enemy fast and with deadly accuracy.

"Your last two crew members are people Jewels knows well, considering they are ex-anchors."

179

Jeremy turned to Manroe. "Ex-anchors? I thought Jewels' disability drained our powers to the point we couldn't use them again?"

"We thought so too until some of our medical healers began doing research and found that your abilities aren't gone. What you do lose is your shielding power. Not your normal psionic shield, but the ability to extend it to another is unusable. Any other gifts you have still remain. They are unaffected."

"Wow. When did you discover this?" Jeremy felt a little betrayed by the news. Imagine how much less stress if he had known he wouldn't become useless after giving up his anchor position!

"We've known for about seven years, thanks to Eric and Skylar's dedication and cooperation."

"And silence," Jeremy snarled, giving Skylar an angry glare.

Skylar shrugged. "You're my best friend, Jeremy, but confidentiality agreements are a pain to get around."

Jeremy nodded and turned to Manroe. "You could have at least told Jewels. Do you realize how agonizing it is for her to believe she's killing her anchors?"

"It was a calculated risk. Besides, if everything works out, the anchor program will be shelved."

"Meaning?" Eric demanded.

"Just what I said," Manroe replied and smoothly changed the subject. "Eric is your diplomat and first contact guide. Skylar is your Intel operative. Now that you're all acquainted, get moving. Your ride is here. Please go down to the loading bay. The fleet is launching and you need to be at the forefront. Colonel Brion has gone to get Jewels and will rendezvous with you. Oh, by the way, the President will be onboard watching. He's going to determine if we're worth all that extra funding. No pressure."

"Sure, no pressure," Jeremy snapped. He turned his back on Manroe. "All right people, let's move out."

Eagerly, the psionics left with Jeremy in the lead.

Chapter 32

Jewels stumbled as her surroundings solidified. They were in a dense rain forest filled with animal sounds. She stepped back and as far away from Adam as possible. She wished Dex was here instead of this creepy human. The thought startled her. When had she started viewing others as human? She knew that answer. It was the moment she'd laid eyes on Dex that her entire existence had irrevocably changed.

"So, pretty lady. When do we start?" Adam took a step in her direction and she moved farther away.

"I don't know. Whenever they decide to begin."

"I have an idea of what we can do while we wait."

Her eyes narrowed at his words. She saw the leer and became more alert. She was at a disadvantage. Adam's mind was shielding hers. However, she could keep him out of her thoughts long enough to make a break for it. "I think not." she broke into a run and plunged into the undergrowth.

She heard Adam cursing as he gave chase. No way was she letting him near her. As she went deeper into the bushes, a thought occurred to her that nearly stopped her in her tracks. She wasn't hearing any thoughts. Not even Adam's. She reached out with her telepathy and touched the mental shield around her mind.

Jewels gasped, disbelief freezing her in place. It wasn't Adam's shield she felt. It was Dex's vibrant and comforting shielding that protected her from the loud thoughts of living things. "Oh, Dex, how did you do it?" she murmured.

"Got you!"

Jewels screamed as she was bowled over by Adam's larger form. They rolled and pain exploded along her back as she slammed into a rock. Adam landed on top of her. Tears filled her eyes and she gasped, frantically trying to quell the agony racing through her. "Get off!" she yelled and slapped him hard.

Adam snarled and grabbed her wrists in a bruising grip. She bucked, trying to dislodge him, but he anticipated her move and backhanded her, making her head ring and her vision swim.

"Stupid, girl! Did you think you could escape me? You're prey and I always catch what I'm hunting. You reek of that stupid Gatoan. Oh, Prince Dex, save me," Adam mocked in a high shrill tone. "He's not going to save you because he's going to be dead! He, his Father and all the other mangy cats that came with them."

"No! You lie!"

Adam leaned in and nuzzled her neck. Jewels let out a disgusted yelp and turned her head away.

"Better learn to like this. You're my prize for being stuck on this godforsaken planet for the last two decades."

"Decades?" Jewels distrusted his words. He was too chatty. That meant either he was just that crazy or he was secure in his plan. Both were bad for her. "You can't be a day over 35," she scoffed.

"Why thank you, Jewels. Try 70 of your Earth years. I volunteered to assist the Lupines in exchange for them helping me become more than a second-rate psionic. Of course, it meant making some sacrifices."

She had a bad feeling about this turn in the conversation. "Sacrifices?"

"Yes, I had to agree to send them psionics for study. It was easy enough. I never had anyone respect my psionic gifts until I met the Lupines. You see, they aren't psionic, but they were hoping to find some way to either breed it into their line or induce it in existing pack members."

"You bastard! How many of us did you send to them? And how did you not get caught?" Angrily Jewels twisted beneath his bulk, determined to get free and kick his sorry behind.

"The Gatoans aren't the only ones with tech-savvy. The Lupines invented gates that do the same thing as a teleport, except they don't rely on human power. They are strategically placed on Earth and throughout the galaxies the Lupines visit."

Jewels couldn't believe what she was hearing. "What was your reward for turning traitor?"

"I get to rule Earth as Bonebreaker's human representative."

She started laughing, she couldn't help it. "You are an idiot, Adam! Do you think these Lupines will honor their word? Do you think you are the only one they are using like this?"

"I know they will keep their word. Yes, they are users, but I'm not stupid enough not to have backup plans," came his smug reply.

"Then you are a fool!"

Adam leaned in closer to her face. "No, not a fool. Besides the job comes with perks. They gave me a little extra boost."

Jewels shivered at the madness in his eyes. "What do you mean?" She wanted to use her abilities, but the Phase Three simulation restricted her powers to telepathy only in order to gauge and test her partner's abilities.

"This." His face morphed and Jewels screamed as Adam's human features disappeared and reformed. Denial hit, but she knew what he had become. It shouldn't be possible, such things were a myth.

"Werewolf," she gasped, going completely still beneath him. Fascinated and repulsed, Jewels simply stared up at him.

Adam placed his muzzle near her cheek and nipped her. She yelped and jerked her head away, feeling blood on her face. "You bit me you, crazy freak!"

"I am not a freak!" He howled.

She wasn't sure how Adam could speak when his face was mostly muzzle and fur. It clicked then what the Lupines must be. "Wolves! You mean the Lupines are wolves?"

::Brilliant deduction. Now, how about I feast on your fear and make you scream?::

Jewels shut her eyes. She was not going to scream for him. His fetid breath blew in her face and then Adam howled in surprise. His weight was gone and she opened her eyes. It took a few seconds to process the fight happening before her.

She recognized Colonel Brion's large form as he fired at Adam who nimbly dodged the blasts.

185

::Get up girl! Use your electrokinesis now!::

Jewels' mouth fell open. The Colonel was psionic! She hadn't sensed it the first time they met. Confused she stood up and called forth the electricity. The familiar pops and crackles brought a not-so-nice smile to her face. "Feast on this, Doggy Face!"

She pulled back her hand and flung an electric blast that slammed into Adam's head and dropped him writhing and howling to the ground. She sprinted over to Colonel Brion's side.

"Sir, what is going on?"

"No time to talk, Lieutenant. We have to get you to the ship. And as for this cur," Brion fired one laser shot into Adam's twitching body. Adam convulsed and stopped moving.

Jewels grimaced, but was relieved. She hadn't relished the idea of becoming dinner. "Ship?"

Brion jogged toward a narrow path and Jewels was forced to run to keep up with him. "Sir! Ship?"

"Yes, Earth's pride and joy. It's named after you, Lieutenant."

"What, me? Why? You're not making sense! This has got to be the craziest Choosing I've ever experienced!"

"It will be your last," Brion informed her.

"What is that supposed to mean?" Jewels halted and stared at the shuttle that sat in the clearing. It wasn't a type she was familiar with.

"You will see, Lieutenant. Now, get in."

Brion ran inside and after a moment's hesitation, so did Jewels.

"Take that seat. I'll explain on the way."

"Way? Where are we going?" she demanded, tired of the half

186

answers.

"To save your husband and our planet."

Jewels sat back in the chair and massaged her aching temples. She felt the vibrations of the engines powering up and they were airborne. Could her life get any stranger?

Chapter 33

Lastbite stared at the screen at the planet called Earth. One puny pathetic Gatoan flagship was in orbit around the blue planet. Laughable.

"Report," he snarled.

"Beta Lastbite, we are reading no other ship signatures."

"And our informant?"

"We've lost his signal. It is no longer on Earth."

"What does that mean?" Lastbite demanded.

"We're not sure. We're checking on it."

"This is ridiculous. Unless...Navigation scan this area again on all bands."

"Yes, Beta Lastbite."

Lastbite had a feeling that he'd missed something important. "Well?"

"Nothing, Beta Lastbite."

"Hail them. I wish to speak to the great King Renten LoudRoar."

"Message sent and received. Vid is live and open."

The screen flickered and was replaced with Renten LoudRoar's leonine face. Lastbite stood and studied the Gatoan King's expression. He saw the craftiness in the other male's eyes. The feeling of a trap surfaced once more. He tamped it down. He was in control here.

"King Renten LoudRoar. I would say a pleasure to meet you, but

I'm afraid that isn't true. I am here to accept your surrender and to retrieve the human female, Jewels Enbran."

Renten rubbed his chin. "And you are?"

"Lastbite, Beta to Alpha Bonebreaker."

"Ah, so once again Bonebreaker sends an inept underling to challenge me. Really, you would think he would have outgrown that by now."

Inept? Lastbite clenched his fist, raised his muzzle and bared his fangs. Stupid cats. They would tremble at the Lupines' might. "Maybe he knows that you are nothing more than a joke and easily defeated by an 'inept underling.' No matter. You will die and we will triumph."

"You sound so sure. Hmm, I wonder. Could it be that you aren't confident at all?" Renten goaded.

"You will not sway me. I will assume that all this talking is to disguise your lack of prowess. I will take great pleasure in ending your miserable lives and subjugating the humans. Good-bye, Gatoan," Lastbite spat and terminated the feed.

"Power up our weapons. It is time to teach the cats respect." Lastbite sat down with a grin. Finally, he would be able to vent his frustration by using the Gatoans for target practice.

"Weapons powered, Beta Lastbite."

"Fire!"

* * *

"Father, maybe you shouldn't have taunted the mutt," Dex

admonished from his seat at the weapons console.

"Perhaps, but we have to make a stand. No more running. We have a right to our lives too!" Renten threw back his head and roared loud and proud. "For honor! For our homes!"

"They're firing!"

"Evasive maneuvers now! Return fire. Try to keep between them and Earth," Renten ordered.

Their ship began a slow roll to dodge the enemy's weapons.

"Communications, have our other three ships join the attack from behind the enemy. We need to split the ships up."

"Message sent and received, Sire."

"Returning fire. We scored a hit on the lead dreadnought. Minor damage," Dex reported.

"Swing us around and target their engine section. If we can disable them, it will make life a little easier," Renten replied.

He looked over at Dex and saw the tension bubbling beneath his focused facade. His son was worried about his missing mate. Renten hoped that for Dex's sake that the human female survived. This was going to be a short fight if the humans didn't come soon. If he had to die, then at least it would be with his head held high and pride for a glorious death. Renten's one regret -- not destroying their enemies sooner.

Chapter 34

"Okay, let me get this straight. My Choosing is over and Dex is my new anchor?"

"Yes, Lieutenant."

"That is fine by me. Now, you're saying you want me to fly our new, shiny, out-of-the-box spaceship using my psi-implant? Are you insane! I'm not a cybernetic psionic. I don't interface with electronics. The psi-implant is used to monitor my health, not do anything else."

"You're placing limits on yourself. Stop that. Let me put it to you this way, young lady. If you don't use that very gifted mind and talents we gave you, we will all die. Do you want that to happen? Even your precious Gatoan husband will be killed."

"Dex," Jewels whispered, her heart giving a painful squeeze at the thought of losing him. "No, I won't let that happen! I still can't believe Psi Ops manipulated my DNA, and right now, I don't care. Understand this, after I'm finished kicking wolf butt, I'm done. I'm not going to stay on Earth. I'm going with Dex to wherever he decides to take me. And you can't stop me."

"Fair enough. Are you ready? The *Jewels II* is over there," Brion gestured out the left window.

"Wow," Jewels whispered and stared at the large, sleek ship. She wasn't much on spacecraft, but even she could tell this vessel packed some power. She gulped and thought about becoming one with the

191

ship. That's how Brion described it. For Dex and Jeremy, who mattered most to her, she would do as Brion asked. It was her turn to keep the men in her life safe. She missed the secretive smile Brion cast in her direction as she prepared to do the impossible.

"We're docking now," he announced. The shuttle jolted a little as it glided into place.

Jewels heard the clang of the docking clamps and the door opened. She stared as the President stuck his head inside.

"Brion! Took you long enough. The Gatoans are getting pounded. Two of their four ships have been disabled. I'm sending out two squadrons right now to assist." The President turned to Jewels. "Don't just sit there, girl! Get up and follow me. We have your seat warm and ready."

Jewels flinched, stood and followed the President from the shuttle. The ship was huge and she didn't have time to get her bearings as she was escorted to the elevator. She fidgeted on the way up and practically ran out into the command center when the doors opened. She tried to take in the entire area and failed. It was huge, oval shaped and in the middle was a giant metallic seat with cables running down the back of it and disappearing into the floor.

Flaring outward from the main seat were four large consoles each with three seats behind it. Stationed in each chair was a psionic that she recognized or had worked with in the past ten years, including two ex-anchors. She did a double take. Shock hit her first, followed by denial and then anger.

"Is this someone's idea of a joke?" she snarled and whirled around to glare at the President.

"Joke?"

Jewels ignored the President's stony expression. "You have two of my former anchors here. If I understood Colonel Brion's explanation, this ship responds to psionics. Any anchors that worked with me in the past would be burned out."

"Ah, I see. Colonel, if you would do the honors."

"Of course, Mr. President. Lieutenant, I am happy to inform you that your power is not lethal as we once thought it to be. You can thank Skylar and Eric for helping our psi-doctors discover that what you drained wasn't an anchor's natural abilities, but their power to shield. Any other gifts they possessed before the pairing, they retained."

She paled and her gaze went from Brion to Skylar and Eric, who both had the grace to flush under her angry scrutiny. "I...see." She felt the tension rise in the room and she didn't care.

Jewels rarely got worked up, but at the moment she felt like making an exception. She wanted to lash out and hurt everyone for not being truthful with her. It was the only thing she ever asked of those she considered friends and comrades. She felt betrayed. Her attention shifted when she saw Jeremy emerge from beneath the console between Skylar and Eric.

Jeremy stood up, dusted his hands off and chuckled. "Jewels! Hey Kid, how about you sit in that seat and let's kick some alien tail!" He slid into the center seat between the two ex-anchors and looked at her expectantly.

Nonplussed, Jewels wavered between giving vent to her frustration or obeying Jeremy's cheerful yet admonishing order. Habit and training won out. She moved toward her seat.

The psionics cheered and Jewels decided that her very long talk with Psi-Ops command would have to wait until later. No one lied to her. No one!

All eleven psionics brushed against her mind and introduced themselves to her once again.

::First Sergeant Patrice Riley reporting as ordered.::

::Hi, Patrice! I haven't spoken to you in ages. How is your son?::

::Oh, you know how he is. Five years old and thinks he's grown.::

Jewels chuckled. *::It's really good to see you again.::*

::Likewise, Jewels. Likewise.::

::Lance Corporal Robin Van Dyke here and glad to see you again, Lieutenant::

::Thank you Robin. Looks like congratulations on the promotion.::

::I told them I didn't want to move up in rank, but I guess when you take a bullet for an officer that means something.::

::Did it hurt?::

::Like the dickens, but I got to play hero so chalk up one mark for the nerd team.::

Jewels giggled and focused on the rest of the introductions.

::Dr. Yasmine Fores. I will be keep track of everyone's health, specifically yours and Colonel Lingley.::

::Duly noted.:: Jewels nodded. She understood what the good doctor was saying and it irked her. Once again she felt like a lab rat, running through a Psi-Ops maze.

::I'm Dr. Melinda Reed. We met once when you were six. Dr. Cosmit is my sister.::

::I thought you looked familiar. It is a pleasure to meet you.::

The male psionics decided to keep it brief, only announcing their names in quick succession.

::Captain Michael Stein::

::Major Nathan Retton::

::Lieutenant Colonel Skylar Anderson::

::Lieutenant Colonel Eric Perez::

::Major Tyler Nonan::

::Captain Lionel Jamison::

::Lieutenant Colonel Malcolm Smith::

Jewels was mollified somewhat. The psionics before her were good people and she felt wanted, welcomed and in control. She stepped up to the command chair and sat. The chair molded itself to her body and she felt the head rest adjusting. She had no warning before the interfacing needle plunged into the back of her neck and connected with her sub-dermal psi-implant.

She yelped as pain lanced through her mind and she forgot to breathe. Her body convulsed and Jewels fell into what she privately thought of as her psionic wellspring where her powers resided.

::Easy, Jewels. Don't force it.::

::That's easy for you to say, Jeremy! You're not the one with a needle being jabbed into your neck!::

::Kid, the system's interface was designed for you. Focus on the vid-screen and react, yet do so with caution. The machine is intuitive

and capable of learning, but dead is still dead if you overreact to anything. We are all here to assist you and to use our unique abilities to save humankind. Your mind now has the downloads of our psi-profiles. Command us, Jewels. We are ready.::

::Thank you, Jeremy.:: She was enveloped by eleven reassuring mental touches. *::Let's go!::*

The ship responded easily to her will as they flew from orbit and headed toward the fight. Jewels felt a ferocity bubbling beneath her normal emotional calm. Dex had named her his Onugrass and she would prove his words true.

Chapter 35

"Jewels, we're approaching the fleet," Lionel announced from the nav-station.

"I see them."

"Incoming feeds from the squadron leaders," Tyler called.

The vid screen split into four panels. She noted with surprise that General Zenath, General Hinson and Colonel Manroe each occupied a panel with a view of the enemy fleet remaining in the center panel.

"Oh, hello." Jewels was a little intimidated by the three men. They all outranked her. She would have come to attention, but the interface chair didn't allow for movement. "We are here, sirs."

"We are yours to command," General Zenath spoke first. The other men nodded.

Jewels couldn't hide her surprise this time. Her mouth fell open. "Me?" she squeaked. "I don't know anything about spacecraft and fighting!"

"Perfect time to learn. Besides, you know more than you think," Manroe replied cheerfully.

Jewels grimaced and closed her eyes. Her head was starting to pound. She almost asked for something to relieve the headache, and stopped when realization dawned. This headache wasn't a stress headache, but rather, a ' data dump' headache. She glared at the screen.

"You just gave me the knowledge, didn't you, Colonel Manroe?"

Her eyes narrowed in fury at the Colonel's high-handedness.

"You will do fine. Like they say, 'knowledge is power,' so use it wisely, Lieutenant."

Jewels pondered the situation and, after a moment, had a strategy. "Here is what we need to do. Split off and try to draw two enemy ships each. Will our weapons do the job, Sir?" Jewels looked at Manroe.

"Yes. And more. Show no fear and no mercy," Manroe advised her.

"As much as this chitchat is inspiring, they're coming!" Jeremy interrupted.

"Evasive maneuvers!"

Jewels didn't have to be told twice. The ship responded to her mental commands and they swerved, avoiding the oncoming enemy fire.

"Return fire!" she ordered.

She was getting the hang of using the interface. It was like the simulators at the Psi-Ops training facilities. Jewels treated the vessel like it was her and she felt the shift in the ship's responses. It was the third pass that allowed them to destroy the dreadnought.

"Yes! Two more to go."

"Jewels, the Gatoan's flagship is in trouble!"

"Oh, no! Dex!" She ignored the yells of her crew as she violently slingshot them around an enemy ship and headed toward the two dreadnoughts firing on the Gatoan ship.

Jewels was seeing red. They were hurting him! She would protect Dex!

"Die, bastards!" The hum of the ship changed to a loud whine and

198

then an energy blast roared from the *Jewels II*, slamming outward in every direction, hitting the dreadnoughts engaged by human ships. The explosions rocked the *Jewels II* and the rest of the human fleet veered to avoid the debris. The enemy ships firing on Dex's vessel were caught in the blast as well. The smaller dreadnought exploded while the one with red markings took only a glancing shot before veering away.

Jewels wasn't worried about anyone else. Her focus was on the Gatoan flagship. She maneuvered her ship in front of theirs.

"Arm weapons and prepare to fire," she snarled as she faced the last remaining dreadnought.

She was panting hard and the center had gone eerily silent.

"Jewels?" Jeremy stood and came to her side.

She didn't answer him. "On screen!" The current battlefield view was replaced by King Renten's face on the left and a giant wolf creature on the right.

"State your name so that I know what to write on your grave!" she snarled at the enemy.

::Jewels, calm down! Don't give him an advantage!:: Jeremy warned.

::I know what I'm doing. Trust me.::

The Lupine sneered. "You're the one the fuss is about? Unbelievable! I am Beta Lastbite. You may have won today, but you will see me again. You humans have made a mistake siding with our enemy. I will take pleasure in watching you fall when they do."

"Yeah, I'm sure you will. It won't be today. Don't come back. Oh,

199

Beta Lastbite?" Jewels' smile was feral. She liked the fear she saw in the Lupine's eyes. "My name is Jewels Enbran-LoudRoar and if you ever cross my path again or try to kill my mate, you will die. Have a nice day." She terminated the vid-link. They watched as the dreadnought powered up its engines and shot off into space.

"Well, damn, Jewels!" Jeremy whistled.

"What? We have to be badder than him. Otherwise we're nothing. That's how wolf packs work on Earth at any rate. The alpha wolf enforces his will on the pack. Betas are secondary. He's not the one we have to worry about. It's the Alpha pulling his strings."

"True. But hey, let's get back to Earth and celebrate. And I happen to know of an anxious cat waiting to see you."

Jewels blushed. "Don't start, Jeremy!"

He held up his hand and laughed. "I wouldn't dream of it."

Jewels giggled and blushed when the other psionics erupted with cheers.

After the celebrating died down, she smiled. "Let's go home."

With only a thought, she turned the ship around and headed to Earth.

Chapter 36

On the Gatoan ship, there was much rejoicing. Only minor injuries had been suffered. Dex saw his father's relief and it made him happy. Amidst the celebrating, he slipped from the bridge and headed to the scout bay.

::Leaving, my son?::

::Yes, Father. I must go planetside. She is waiting for me. I will be bringing her with us.::

::I thought you might wish to do so. Is she all right with that?::

::Yes, Father, she is. My little human has spirit.::

::Of that, I have no doubt. Go, then, my son. Fetch your mate and bring her home.::

::Thank you, Father.::

Dex reached the bay and quickly boarded the shuttle. He impatiently paced as they flew to the Fort Blackwater base. He thought about the battle. His heart had been in his throat when he'd felt Jewels' mind right before she demolished all but the lead Lupine dreadnought.

When Jewels had appeared on the screen, his heart filled with pride as she stood up to the enemy. Now he wanted to hold her in his arms and make sure she was truly all right. He needed to breathe her scent and feel her mind link with his.

The door opened and he hurried down the ramp. He scanned the area that was filled with excited celebrating humans. He felt Jewels' mind first and then he spotted her. Jewels was running across the courtyard with a huge smile on her face.

Dex roared and the crowd parted as he ran down the middle toward her.

::Jewels! My little human!:: Dex cried and caught her easily when she leaped into his arms and smothered his face in kisses.

::Never, ever leave me! I want to be with you always,:: Jewels ordered.

She was trembling and he hugged her hard. He saw her tears and licked away the salty drops from her face. *::I will never leave you, my mate. My little human. Always and forever. You truly are a gem to me.::*

::And I wouldn't have it any other way,:: Jewels added and kissed him hard.

Both their minds, hearts and souls were at last together and Dex felt at peace.

::Come, let me show you how much I need you,:: Jewels whispered, her violet eyes focused on Dex's green ones.

::Oh? And what does my little Onugrass have in mind?::

::I don't know. Maybe something like this,:: she purred and sent him a flurry of images of what she wanted to do to him.

He growled eagerly, thoroughly enjoying this playful side of her. *::I do believe I like the way your mind works.::*

::Thought you might.:: Jewels abruptly grew quiet and Dex realized the other humans were staring. *::Let's go some place quiet.::*

He caught the picture of a beach in her thoughts and without waiting, teleported them there. Dex felt her surprise and relief.

"Thank you, my prince, I always feel like a freak when so many people gawk at me." Jewels snuggled closer to him and closed her eyes.

He felt an undercurrent of emotional pain from her and he wondered. He decided to ask later and held her tightly, breathing in her scent.

Dex loosened his hold and gently kissed her upturned face. He stroked her cheek and she glanced up at him. "You are safe, Jewels, but if you ever again pull a stunt as you did during the battle today, I will show you how dominant my will is," he warned.

Jewels' eyes widened and then she glared at him. "Oh, no. I refuse to deal with the 'I'm Alpha Male. Bow down and scrape.' I'm fully capable, your Highness, of defending myself and those I love."

He sighed. "Jewels, my little warrior, I know you can. For my peace of mind, let me take care of you. I am your mate and your anchor. Trust me to keep you safe."

Dex knew this moment was crucial. He had read the detailed file on Jewels that the President had given them two days ago. Jewels had overcome much. Yet despite everything, she still fought. He loved that bravery.

Jewels stared at her feet before turning her gaze on him. The vulnerability in her eyes shook him and he sucked in a breath, prepared to say more if it would help her comprehend the depth of his determination to make her happy.

"Dex, I've waited a long time for a man that would love me as I am and not be afraid of my powers. I wanted a man to be strong so that if I got weak he could hold me up. I grew up knowing that my anchors were never going to be permanent. That's why Jeremy was such a surprise. Five years and when he said his gift was almost exhausted...."

"Jewels," Dex whispered, unhappy that she was sad. He reached out a paw and wiped away her tears that had started to fall. "I feel the depth of your loneliness. Did you tell any of your anchors this?"

She shook her head. "I was too little to understand, but once I got older and learned the name for the emotion, I was too accustomed to hiding it. Besides, when working for the military, you never let them know you have emotional issues. It's the fastest way to either get booted or earn a reputation as a loony."

Dex hated feeling useless, but he wasn't sure what to do. He would never understand the complexities of humans. It was time to change topics. "I do not pretend to know how it felt, but I hope, my little human, that one day I will. Right now, I wish to mate with you."

Her feminine response to his seductively purred words were immediate. Her arousal scent rose sharply and he grinned. He gently tugged her to him and rubbed his cheek against hers. He chuckled when Jewels giggled.

"Dex, your whiskers tickle!"

"Yes, and I will be tickling other parts of you very soon, my human Onugrass."

Jewels sucked in a breath and her fingers wrapped in the fur on his arms.

He leaned in and whispered, "My precious gem, care to tangle with me?" He licked a slow, sensual path from her ear to her neck.

"Yes!"

Her eagerness was amazing and Dex was happy to oblige. He reached up to undo her hair tie, wanting to see her hair free.

::Um, hmm. Sorry to interrupt you two lovebirds, but we have a situation happening here and I need you back immediately.::

::You know, Colonel Lingley, your timing is atrocious.:: Dex snapped.

::Sorry, your Highness, duty before pleasure. You two must get back here right now.::

"Dex? Dex, why did you stop?" Jewels complained.

He blinked and focused on Jewels' concerned face. "You didn't hear him?"

"Hear, who?" Jewels peered about. "I don't see anyone. Dex, are you all right?"

Dex pondered this unexpected turn of events. "You didn't hear Colonel Lingley's telepathic summons?"

"No," she replied slowly and then she paled.

"Jewels?"

She pulled away from him and backed up two steps.

"Jewels?" Dex repeated and reached for her, but she shook her head.

"No, Dex, stay there for a moment."

Baffled, he watched her close her eyes. After a moment, Jewels opened them and her panicked expression raised his protective instincts.

"Jewels, what is it?"

"Dex, I can't hear anything."

"I do not understand." Her hearing seemed to be working fine. After all, she'd just responded to his question.

"I don't mean with my ears. I can't 'hear' anything telepathically. Not even the insects buzzing about. There is silence except when I touch your mind. What has happened to me? What is going on?" she demanded.

Comprehension dawned and Dex frowned. "You cannot sense any psionics?"

"That's right, only you," she grumbled.

"Is that such a bad thing?" he teased.

"No...Maybe. What if I need help and you are out of range? If I can't 'hear' another that could save me, I'll end up dead."

"Good point. Look, Jeremy said they have some situation and that he needs us back. We will have to deal with this later."

"Agreed. Shall I do the honors?" She took his paw in her hand.

"Yes, my mate, I will not rob you of your entrance."

"Thank you, Dex." She stroked his fur and he rewarded her with a loud purr. She grinned and teleported them to the base.

Chapter 37

He had failed. Lastbite couldn't believe it. Not only had the humans proven an unexpected factor, but their technology was more advanced than the Lupine hybrid had led the Alpha to believe. He shouldn't have lost. Ten dreadnoughts to four puny Gatoan ships. It should have been easy pickings.

The humans had arrived and inflicted damage. That hadn't worried Lastbite. No, what bothered him was the red-haired human female that piloted the human flagship and destroyed his fleet.

When she appeared on-screen, he'd been astonished and furious. That pathetic hybrid Adam boasted of his prowess, but obviously lacked the skills necessary to contain one little female. It was amazing that the female known as Jewels commanded such respect.

"Beta Lastbite, we are nearing the galactic gate."

"What?" he snarled when the smaller male cowered.

"My Beta, we have located the hybrid Adam. He is dead."

"I guessed as much. Where is the signal coming from?"

"A space station in orbit around Jupiter."

"Any life readings onboard?"

"No, my Beta."

"Retrieve the body. Perhaps in death he'll be more useful than in life."

"Yes, my Beta."

Lastbite sat back and considered his next move. Bonebreaker did not tolerate loss. He had to be prepared to fight his Alpha if he wished to live. All of this was Dex's fault. That disgusting Gatoan prince was a thorn in Lastbite's side, one he was going to remove. First, he had to survive his Alpha. "I will pay you back tenfold, Dex, for what you've cost me."

He would make this work and he would be victorious. There was no other option. The bowing and scraping were over. He would be Alpha and his enemies would tremble. Yes, they would.

* * *

Jewels and Dex appeared outside the base's command center. She was still perturbed that she couldn't sense other psionics. True, she wanted to be able to shield her mind from thoughts, but not at the expense of becoming telepathically deaf.

::*Mate, you are glowering.*::

::*I am not, Dex.*:: At his pointed look, she sighed. ::*All right, maybe a little. I don't like not being able to tell where others are.*::

He put his arm around her and hugged her. ::*I am here, and will keep you safe.*::

::*Thanks, just what I need, a cat in shiny armor.*:: Jewels hated to sound peevish, but the unsettled feeling remained.

"Jewels! Dex! This way," Jeremy called from the doorway.

She slipped free of Dex's embrace and jogged over to her former anchor. "Jeremy, we have to..."

"...Talk. Yes, I know, but not out in the open. Come inside where it's shielded."

She nodded and went in. Jewels knew that Dex would follow. She could feel his displeasure at her eagerness to leave his side. She'd worry about his ego later. She needed to focus on herself.

They were met by Elenora who stood with med-scanner and data-pad in hand. "Good, you made it. Jewels, please sit on the bio-bed."

"Why?"

"Because it's an order, Lieutenant," Jeremy barked.

Jewels twitched, threw him a petulant glare and did as instructed.

::My Onugrass, sheath your claws. They are both concerned for you.::

::I don't need pity!::

::Jewels, it is not pity, only worry. Perhaps they have the answers we seek.::

::I hope you're right.:: She fought the urge to fidget during the medical scan. She didn't feel like being scolded.

"What's the verdict, Elenora?"

"It's what I thought, Jeremy, but this second set of scans proves it."

"Proves what?" Jewels demanded.

"That your mental bond with Dex is so tightly connected that severance of it will result in death for both of you."

Dex's growl of surprise echoed Jewels' own shock. "Why would we sever our bond? We just found each other. I was hoping for long life, happiness, etc. Unless you know something I don't? Or you had other plans?" She focused on Dex, unsure of his true intentions.

"Do you have so little faith in me, my human Onugrass? My people mate for life. However, I've never heard of a mate bond that would result in death for both if one died."

Jewels paled. "Oh great. I knew it! I really am a freak!"

"Jewels, you are not a freak and if you say that again, big bad cat husband or not, I will put you over my knee and tan your backside!"

She stared at Jeremy's furious expression. He had that I-mean-business look. She decided that meekness was the better part of valor. "Sorry. I won't say it any more, Jeremy. I'm afraid, ok? First my loss of telepathic hearing, and now the possibility of death if Dex dies is a bit much to handle."

"What do you mean loss of telepathic hearing?" Elenora demanded.

"Apparently, she can't 'hear' anyone's mind except mine."

"Oh, is that all?"

Jewels spun around and glared at the newcomer. "Colonel Manore! Why are you here? No, wait let me guess. You're my own personal little doom cloud come to rain on my head? Well, sorry, you'll have to get in line!"

"Jewels!" Jeremy growled.

Manroe held up a hand. "Colonel Lingley, it's all right. She's allowed to be angry, but really, young lady, you need to relax. Maybe another roll in the sack with your handsome feline will calm you down."

"Why you arrogant...." She lunged for him and was snagged by Dex who securely wrapped his arms around her, pinning her against his body.

"I like that male's idea," he whispered in her ear.

Jewels blushed and closed her eyes. She knew when she was defeated. "What did you mean by your comment?"

"Your ability will come back. Right now your mind is adjusting to Dex as your anchor and as your mate. It's suffered a double whammy, if you will, and, so to cope, shut down one avenue of your power."

"How long will it last, Colonel? My people have nothing like this."

"Not sure. It varies from person to person. Minimum is two months."

"Two months!" Jewels wailed, horrified at the thought of not having her abilities at full strength.

"And the longest?"

"We've had only one case where it was permanent."

"That should be a 'need to know.' You should tell psionics what happens when we find our one and only," she snarled at Manroe.

"Really? And have them all react like you did? I think not, Lieutenant. Besides, if you had known, you wouldn't have bonded with the Prince because of fear of the loss. It works much better this way. Now, I have a more pressing matter to discuss with the pair of you."

"Lovely, we're all ears."

"Sarcasm is not needed, Lieutenant. I am on my way to meet with the Psi-Ops Council. They want a full report on what has happened here. They will also decide that you will not to be allowed to leave the planet."

"What! They can't do that!" Jewels shouted and squirmed hard until Dex set her on her feet. "I have a right to be with my husband. I am not property!"

"I agree. So here is what I am going to do. I will report as ordered. You two will stay here. I will call Prince Dex to come and explain his position on the matter. Your Highness, I would advise you to use every ounce of power and command you have in you to make an impressive showing. It is the only way that they will back down."

Jewels studied Manroe's face. "You already know how this is all going to end, don't you?"

"Not really. You still have free will. That always changes the flow of possibilities. Is everyone clear on what we are doing?"

"Yes, we're clear."

"Good. I must go. Remember, Prince Dex, be ready." Manroe's form became transparent and then he was gone.

"He is an interesting human," Dex commented as he walked over to Jeremy.

"That's not the word I'd use, but he's very good at what he does.," Jewels muttered. "So what do we do now?"

"Well, Kid, we wait. That's all we can do until Manroe calls." Jeremy shrugged.

"That's just peachy." Jewels stalked toward the nearest chair and sat down. She hoped that Manroe did not fail. She couldn't contemplate a life without Dex.

Chapter 38

Renten was pleased that the enemy had been defeated, at least for the moment. Soon the battle would be on his turf and then the mutts would see that a Gatoan was not to be messed with. All around the ship his people were celebrating their victory, one that would not have been possible without the humans. They had been the deciding factor.

Happy with his thoughts, he stood and left the bridge. He took the el-lift several floors down to the battle room. He smiled as the warriors roaming the halls stopped to cheer and bow before him. He acknowledged each and every one of them. The battle room was mostly empty when he arrived. Renten spotted Leftclaw in the corner, tapping furiously away on a console.

"Hello, old friend. What are our ships' statuses?"

"My King, the other ships report minor damage. We shall be ready to leave in one Earth day."

"You don't sound pleased, Leftclaw." Renten sat and stared intently at his long-time adviser and friend. "Tell me, what is wrong?"

Leftclaw scowled and he tensed at the Posaima's expression. Leftclaw only got that look when he had to impart distasteful news.

"Your Majesty, while you were negotiating with the humans, I went to check on the Queen as you commanded."

Renten's eyes narrowed. "Go on."

"I found the Queen with one of your guardsmen. She was very

much enjoying his...attentiveness."

Renten stared blankly, the words not registering at first. The explanation sunk in and he surged to his feet with a roar of denial and rage.

"Your Majesty! Please, calm down!" Leftclaw ordered. "Both traitors have been imprisoned and await your judgment. The Queen must be removed from her position. She has violated mate-law and shamed the monarchy with her actions."

Renten shook with fury. Rialla had betrayed him! He had suspected her of infidelity, but had ignored his instincts, blaming his insecurity on having a younger mate. Now he knew the truth and it left a bitterness in his heart.

"I've failed as a mate. I should have done more," he whispered.

"No, your Majesty. You did not fail. She is to blame. She schemed from the start to get what she desired. The only thing you are guilty of is wanting a mate to share your life and rule with."

Leftclaw came around the console to stand by his side. "What do you want to do, Ren?"

Renten threw his friend a startled glance. "You haven't called me that since we were cubs. I will decide punishment once we are home on Felinia. No need to damage the crew's morale. How many know?"

"Only five besides myself. They have been sworn to secrecy. The rest is speculation."

Renten nodded and, with a heavy heart, stood to leave.

Leftclaw placed a paw on his shoulder. "Ren, remember, even kings can make mistakes."

"Thanks for your kind words, old friend, but I was warned about Rialla's ways. I thought that having my wisdom and experience to balance out her willfulness and youth would help her settle down." He sighed and flexed his claws. "I need to return planetside to get my son and his mate. I'm ready to take my leave of Earth."

"As am I, my King. We will weather this as we have other such events."

"Thank you, Leftclaw, for all your support."

"That is what friends do. Now, go, celebrate your son's success on his mate hunt."

"Yes, joy must come before sorrow, and my son has waited long enough for this moment." He smiled at Leftclaw's chuckle and teleported to the base to find Dex.

* * *

Manroe stood outside the double doors that led to the inner chambers of the Psi-Ops Council. Consisting of seven of the most powerful and talented psionics on the planet, the Council set policy for all psionics. He had been offered a seat a few years ago, but declined. He knew his talents were needed elsewhere.

Now he stood there, ready to bring them the report from the Fort Blackwater base. This meeting would be unpleasant because once the Council heard that Jewels and Dex were bonded, chaos would erupt.

"Well, I did warn them this might happen," he muttered before entering the dimly lit room.

It was hard to make out the raised dais with the seven seated figures cloaked in shadows. The current Council had four women and three men on it.

"Colonel Manroe, welcome. You have news for us?"

"Yes, I do. We, along with the Gatoan ships, repelled the Lupine intruders."

"And the girl? How did Lt. Enbran fare with the new interface?"

"It took her a few minutes, but after she settled down, her performance was flawless. She kept our skies safe and clear of the enemy. She deserves our thanks."

"The possibility you saw came true. Congratulations, Colonel, on another successful play. We want Lt. Enbran prepped and ready for her next assignment with the Glascoe Corporation."

"Council members, if I may interrupt for a moment."

"Go ahead, Colonel. Speak your mind."

"I must inform you that Lt. Jewels Enbran is not available for reassignment."

"What?"

"Ladies and gentlemen of the Council, our Lieutenant found her true-bond during this mission."

"Oh, is that all? That is good news. We shall send her true-mate with her."

Manroe cleared his throat. "That will be difficult."

"Difficult, Colonel?"

"Yes, difficult, near impossible, I might add. Her true-mate and new anchor is the Crown Prince Dex LoudRoar of Felinia."

The Council erupted in shouts and protests at his words. Questions were tossed at him so fast he didn't have time to answer them. After a moment, an angry hush fell.

"Colonel, it is your job to watch for possible bondings that might occur. How could you allow this pairing? The Lieutenant is the strongest psionic to be made in the last fifty years. We cannot allow this to stand."

Manroe stiffened. "Let me get this straight. You want their bond broken?"

"Yes, Colonel, that is what we command."

"I see. Well, I have to say, that I respectfully decline this assignment."

"Colonel, this is not a game. You will obey the Council's wishes on this matter."

Manroe laughed and even to his own ears it sounded sinister. "Do you honestly think you can bend me to your will? Me, the one who can see all possibilities? This Council has lost sight of what is important for our survival and that of humans. Lt. Enbran and her mate are crucial for our longevity as a group. We need the Gatoans and I will not allow you to destroy Jewels' happiness."

"How dare you!"

"I dare because I know what will happen if I obey your ridiculous order." He reached up and removed his shades. Manroe knew his eyes were glowing. "I'm warning you now that the time of the Psi-Ops Council is nearing its end. You will either adapt or be swept away in the cleansing."

"Colonel Manroe, stand down!"

Manroe glanced at the far left Council seat. The head of the Council sat there. He knew every member's name, their fears, deceits, and desires, even their hopes and dreams. The leader, though, was special.

"Cassandra, remember what happened the last time the Council meddled with a bond. The outcome led to death for humans and psionics. Do not make the same mistake twice."

He felt the surprise of the remaining six members as they looked to their leader.

Cassandra started clapping, her tone was mocking. "Well played, Colonel. We will allow the bond to stand. Lt. Enbran, however, is not allowed to leave Earth. We need all our assets here. Her true-mate can stay here with her."

"Still a 'no?' See, I knew you would do this too. That's why I have someone you need to meet." Manroe turned and Dex appeared next to him. "Council, let me present Crown Prince Dex LoudRoar of Felinia. I do believe that as Lt. Enbran's husband, he has a say in her future plans."

"Colonel, you are out of line!" Cassandra thundered.

"I don't believe so. Prince LoudRoar, the floor is yours." Manroe stepped back and smirked. This was going to be fun.

Chapter 39

Dex stood proudly before the human psionics and allowed his displeasure to fill the silence.

"I stand before you as a courtesy only. I will be taking my mate, Jewels Enbran, with me when I return to Felinia. I understand how precious she is to you, but her value to me is priceless. I may only be twenty-five of your Earth years, but among my kind that is past the age when we take mates. I was desperate to find my mate. To find her here is a gift, and one I'm thankful for. She completes me and to separate us is to kill us. I will not allow that."

"Do not try to intimidate us, Gatoan, for we deal harshly with threats," the woman at the far right snarled.

Dex studied the female. That one had to be the leader. She radiated fury and.... He sniffed the air. Fear, he smelled fear. He grinned and bared all his teeth. He felt the shift of emotions from certainty to panic on the part of the Council.

"For the good of your world, don't cross me. I will fight to keep Jewels and you will lose in the end."

He stared down each member, saving the female leader for last. "Isn't it better for you that my mate leave with me? You won't have to do anymore Choosings and lose good telepaths because of her disability."

::Well played, Prince Dex, well played.::

219

Dex almost laughed at Manroe's smug telepathic message. *::I thought so too.::*

"What say you, Council?" Manroe demanded.

"Fine! Take her. That girl is nothing but trouble," the leader snapped.

Dex's tail swished back and forth. He really disliked the Council leader. "Thank you for your...understanding in this matter. May our two species continue on this path of friendship and peace." He turned to Manroe. "Coming?"

"You know what, I believe I will."

Dex only grunted before he teleported from the room.

Manroe bowed to the Council. "Always a pleasure."

"One day you will push us too far, Colonel, and there be no rescue for you."

"Perhaps, but that is something I can live with. Good day." He blew Council leader Cassandra a kiss and laughed at her indignant expression as he rippled and vanished from view.

*　　*　　*

Jewels stared at the clock, anxiety filling her heart with each minute that passed. Why wasn't Dex back yet? If Manroe so much as harmed one tuft of fur on Dex, she would rearrange the Colonel's face.

"Hey, Kid, you're going to burn a hole in the clock with your glare," Jeremy chided.

"Sorry! I just have this feeling...." She stiffened, whirled and fell into a defensive crouch. "Jeremy!" she hissed.

He spun and drew his weapon. "What?" His gaze traveled the room.

She froze and stared in shock behind him. "No!" She stumbled backward. "You're dead!"

Adam grinned at her. "You are the fool. I will come for you and your Gatoan Prince. Never pull the wolf's tail unless you can stand the bite." He leered and faded away, leaving Jewels shaken and confused. He should be dead!

"Jewels! Hey, Kid, snap out of it!"

She blinked and Jeremy's face came into focus. "What? Did you see him?"

Jeremy and Elenora exchanged worried glances and Jewels' anger rose. "Don't do that! I hate it when people do that!"

"Do what?"

"You know what I mean, Jeremy! The look that dismisses what I say."

"Jewels, please calm down. We didn't see anyone."

"This isn't happening. I won't let it," she mumbled, disregarding Elenora's plea for calm.

"Won't let what happen, my little human?"

"Dex!" Jewels flung herself into his arms. "Please, tell me we can get out of here?"

"Yes, my mate. Remind me to tread carefully in the future when dealing with your Colonel Manroe."

"He's not my Colonel Manroe, but being wary around him is a

great idea," she said as another figure rippled into view.

"Lieutenant, I'm hurt. After all I went through to secure your release from Psi-Ops, you could show a little more gratitude."

Jewels studied Manroe's expression. She wasn't completely sure he was joking. A nudge from Dex reassured her.

"Thank you, Colonel, for your help. And I do mean that."

"I also wish to add my thanks," Renten stated from the doorway.

Jewels jumped and then smiled sheepishly. Not being able to hear others would take some getting used to. "My King." She dropped into a curtsy.

Renten strolled over and she admired his graceful glide. King Renten knew how to make an entrance. He tapped her on the shoulder.

"Rise, mate to my son. You do not bow or pay homage to me. You are family. I have come to take you both back to the ship. Our people wish to celebrate your joining."

She blushed and stared at her feet.

"I'd never thought I'd see the day that you would be tongue-tied!" Jeremy crowed.

"Shut up, Jeremy! You know I hate ceremonies," Jewels complained.

"Get used to it, Kid. You're royalty now."

She sighed. Jeremy was right. Life would be a lot more interesting in the days to come.

"Come, my little Onugrass. Time to say good-bye. My father and our crew are anxious to leave. We have time to get your belongings and settle into our quarters on the ship before we travel to Felinia."

Jewels stroked Dex's silky fur. Yes, time to go. She straightened and went to Jeremy and Elenora. She hesitated and Jeremy pulled her into his arms. He hugged her hard.

"I'm gonna miss you, Kid. Take care of the big guy, okay?"

She started to cry, but managed a choked, "Yes, Sir."

Jeremy stepped back and Elenora added her own hug. "Don't forget to come back and visit, Jewels. We'll be here."

"Thank you. Both of you." Jewels wiped away her tears. "I'll miss you two the most. I will try to visit when I can. I promise."

"We will make sure she does," Dex agreed.

Jewels moved to stand between Dex and his father. She felt dwarfed, protected.

Colonel Manroe came forward and shook Dex's paw. His parting words were for Jewels. "Safe journey. Until time turns and we see each other again, remember we are only a thought away."

She nodded. "I won't forget." She slid a hand into each Gatoan's paw. "Let's go."

"Good-bye, friends," Dex rumbled.

"Bye!" Jewels' eyes glistened with tears as her last view of Earth was the smiling faces of Jeremy, Elenora and Colonel Manroe.

Chapter 40

Dimitri sat at his desk and stroked his cybernetic arm. He'd been afraid the Lupines would enslave Earth. True, Chris Manroe's possibility matrix had yet to fail, but that didn't make the experience any easier.

He glanced down at the datapad with the report on Maussey. As expected, the man refused to speak. The only statement the soon-to-be former Brigadier General had to say was that they would regret arresting him. No matter. Truth would keep Maussey inside prison for the rest of his life.

Dimitri picked up a different datapad and glared at the information on the screen. The Psi-Ops Council wanted to schedule a meeting to discuss the changes and guidelines that needed to be made now that psionic weaponry had been introduced and was available for use.

"You know, brooding will give you gray hair and wrinkles," Manroe chided from the doorway.

Dimitri sighed and rubbed his temples. "Chris, I swear I'm going to make you wear a proximity beeper."

"Naw, that would take the fun out of sneaking up on you. What's wrong, Mr. President? Aren't you happy with our recent successes? Jewels helped test the new psionic weaponry, Maussey's sorry behind is in jail where it belongs, and we gained the Gatoans as allies. Not too bad, if I do say so myself."

"Yeah, not bad. Don't forget we made an enemy or should I say cemented the Lupines' desire to enslave and kill us. Aren't you tired of this? I mean, how many more times are we going to avert crises like this one? Jewels isn't always going to be able to save our butts."

"Dimitri, do you remember what I told you when we first met twenty-two years ago?"

"You mean the day at the POW camp when I thought I was going to die?"

"Yes, that day."

"You said that we would be best friends and, along with Hinson, Zenath and Brion, would change the world, make it better. Protect the innocent. Be heroes."

"And have I not kept that promise?"

Dimitri studied Chris for a long moment. "Yes, you have. Humanity has changed and matured from those dark days. Yet, I can't help but wonder if we should continue to meddle. Maybe we should just let events run their course."

"That, my friend, is the timeless question that all leaders face. I cannot tell you what to do. However, when considering your options, don't forget the good that has been done."

"Careful, Chris. I might think you've grown a conscience."

Manroe snorted. "You wish. I'm off. So many loose ends and not enough hours in a day to fix every one of them. Be safe, Dimitri. And don't wallow in guilt too long. We need your head in the game. This week was only a test of what is to come. Find the strength to keep going."

"I will take your advice into consideration. Be safe too, old friend."

"Don't I always?" Manroe smirked and rippled from view.

Dimitri glanced at the picture frame. He still had a promise to keep.

* * *

"Dex, this ship is amazing!" Jewels looked in wonder at the huge trees that surrounded the waterfall. "And this is a females-only area?"

"Yes. However, certain king's guardsmen, like myself, are allowed in here. Once our people have gotten used to you, you will spend much of your time here when not with me."

"So you isolate the females from the males?" She frowned. She wasn't sure she liked that idea.

"We are communal in nature, but yes we do separate males and females. When we wish to, as you humans say, 'make love' we find our mates."

"Sounds sexist to me. Look, Dex, you've met my kind. See how we do things. In our culture, mates stay together, not apart. This," she waved her hand about, "is not what I signed on for. If you're too ashamed to be with me, take me back to Earth right now."

He frowned. "I am not ashamed of you, my Onugrass. Why would you think such a thing?"

"Because that's how separating me from you until you need me for a sexual romp, makes me feel. How are we to function as mates and an anchored pair if you toss me in here and throw away the key?" Jewels folded her arms and glared at him.

Dex blushed and his tail swished in agitation. "I never thought of it that way. It is the way we've always done things. I will admit, I like your species' way of doing things better."

"Yeah, go figure. A little communication and togetherness never hurt anyone. And what about children? Where do they stay?"

"Usually with the mother until they are weaned and then they are sent to school."

"That's something at least," Jewels muttered.

"I promise, I will do my best to change things for you. I want you happy," Dex vowed.

"I know, Dex." She stroked his face, relishing the silky feel of his fur against her fingertips. "So, where am I staying on the trip to Felinia?"

"You can stay with me. I do have a room as Prince."

"Good, because right now, I'm wanting a taste of Gatoan." Jewels giggled at his sudden hungry look.

"That's good because I've been craving a certain human beauty," Dex growled and tugged her to him.

She willingly went, a smile filling her face as she pulled his head down and kissed him slowly. She let the heat of her desire spill from her mind to his and felt his eager response.

A cough startled Jewels and she jerked back from Dex, who growled a curse in his native tongue.

Jewels peered around him and noticed a slender Onugrass watching them. "Oh! Sorry, didn't know anyone was in here with us."

Dex turned and stiffened. Jewels glanced between him and the newcomer. She felt the tension and reached for Dex's mind for answers only to be rebuffed when he threw up a mental wall.

Dismayed and a little upset, Jewels inched away from him, placing Dex and the Onugrass in her line of vision and not at her back.

"No apologies needed. I see the rumor is true. Dex mated with a human."

"Nala!"

Jewels blushed and straightened. "Yes, he did. He is an excellent lover."

Nala threw Dex a knowing look and Jewels wanted to strangle the Onugrass. Were the two of them an item before Dex had met her? She was dying to ask him, but he still had his barrier in place.

"I see. My Prince, the King has instructed that I be your mate's helper. I am to assist her in learning more about us and what is expected of the consort to the Prince."

"As my King so orders," Dex replied and bowed.

Jewels wasn't sure what to do so she stood silently by.

"My little Onugrass, I will leave you in Nala's capable hands once we arrive at Felinia. For now, come with me."

"Your Highness!"

Jewels felt a little smug at Nala's shocked expression. *::Chew on that, you little hussy!::* She should have felt remorse for being so jealous, but she wasn't about to let another woman ruin her relationship with Dex.

Oh, he was going to explain exactly what Nala was or had been to

228

him, but that could wait. Right now, she was going to get Dex to his quarters and prove to him that she was Onugrass enough for him.

Dex took her hand and bustled her by the shocked Nala. Neither spoke until they arrived at his room. The door had just closed when Jewels pounced on Dex and knocked him to the floor.

"Who was she?" Jewels demanded while making sure to keep Dex pinned.

"A female with dreams of marrying a prince. Thankfully that option is no longer available to her," he added.

"You two weren't mating with each other, were you?"

Dex stared into her eyes and she squirmed. She didn't want him to see her jealousy, but she had to know.

"No. Until you came along, no female stirred me."

"What? You're joking right?" Jewels was skeptical of that claim.

"I wish I was. Not being able to, 'rise to the occasion,' was an embarrassment for me and my father's bloodlines. If the Heir Apparent cannot reproduce, he is denied the position of King. Knowing that I was the only one with the problem made it worse. I know it hurt my father and I was desperate. I now realize that I was waiting for you."

Jewels felt tears threatening to fall. "I'm glad I could be of some use. Silly males, always have to be difficult."

Dex chuckled and purred beneath her. She felt herself getting aroused. That purr, especially his particular vibration.... She yelped when Dex rolled her beneath him.

"Now, mate, let me show you how much you mean to me."

"Always, my Prince. Always." And she sealed it with a kiss.

Epilogue

Manroe stood on the steps of Psi-Ops HQ and stared up at the starry sky. It seemed strange that only three weeks ago the Earth and her people faced an invasion. He knew that it would all work out. Funny how things had hinged on love.

::Are you still brooding, Manroe?:: Jeremy's voice filled his mind.

Manroe smirked. *::Me, brood? I think you have things confused, brother. I don't brood, I plot.::*

Jeremy stepped up next to him. "Oh, come on, Chris. Even you had to admit that we played that one really close to the vest."

"And you two almost got us killed," growled Brion as he emerged from the shadows and joined them.

"Spoilsport," Jeremy countered. "Admit it, Xavier, we took care of our little sister. We made sure she got her happily ever after."

"You always were a romantic. Besides, she doesn't even know why we helped her."

"You make it sound like it's a bad thing, Xavier."

"Maybe it is. She may be our sibling, but I didn't feel such an urgent need as you two to see her married off. That's precious human DNA being wasted on aliens."

"Not wasted, trust me," Chris stated.

Jeremy stiffened and Xavier looked thoughtful.

"Good evening, brothers. Until we meet again. May the winds of life fly you in the right direction." Manroe smiled at the disgusted glances his siblings gave him. Let them chew on that one for a while. He walked away, whistling a forgotten lullaby.

Author's Notes

I decided to use some current army rankings for my military in *Jewels*.

*The rank of Special Lieutenant is an honorary title bestowed on military psionics with an ability Level 3 or higher and distinguishes them from the regular rank of Lieutenant. The rank grants the psionic certain privileges and leeway in combat. I've included in these notes the ranking order and a listing of the Gatoan family bloodlines.

Military Rank

General (Gen)

Brigadier General (BG)

Colonel (COL)

Lt. Colonel (LTC)

Major (MAJ)

Captain (CPT)

Special Lieutenant (LT)

Lieutenant (LT)

Lance Corporal (LC)

Chief Warrant Officer (CWO)

First Sergeant (1SG)

Sergeant (SGT)

Private (PVT)

Gatoan Bloodlines

High Ruling Family

Onugra (male lion) / Onugrass (female lion)

The Ruling Families

Farsemi (male panther) / Farsemiss (female panther)

Loporfir (male cheetah) / Loporfirass (female cheetah)

Rieyad (male tiger) / Rieyadess (female tiger)

Posaima (male puma) / Posaimass (female puma)

Mezalik (male lynx) / Mezalikiss (female lynx)

Eirarju (male snow leopard) / Eirarjuss (female snow leopard)

Vasdji (male jaguar) / Vasdjiss (female jaguar)

Minor Houses

Zakei (male bobcat) / Zakeiss (female bobcat)

Eyriel (male leopard) / Eyrieluss (female leopard)

Hiesaro (male ocelot) / Hiesaross (female ocelot)

The High Ruling Family, can and has, changed from one bloodline to another. Reasons for the change: no heirs, Royal Challenge, or public outcry.

Moonbeams

Book 1 in the Beams and Light Trilogy

A Veil Recipe

3 clueless college students
1 magical dimension
1 Warrior Princess
A pinch of danger

Take three clueless college students, mix in a tobacco field. Combine one magical dimension and stir in a defiant Warrior Princess. Throw in a pinch of danger and slow cook until steaming.

Invite five angry deities. Open and serve your new heap of trouble.

Now Available!
ISBN-10: 1451559852
ISBN-13: 978-1451559859

Amazon * Kindle Store * Barnes & Noble
Books-A-Million * Google Books
Smashwords.com (all ebook formats)

About the Author

Lakisha Spletzer is a single mother who is inspired by her children to write the adventures in her mind. A native of Coeburn, Virginia, she moved to Citrus County, Florida in 2004 and has enjoyed the warmth ever since.

Lakisha has a Bachelors of Arts in Communications from the University of Virginia-Wise. She teaches dance at Dance Central in Inverness, Florida and works for H & R Block during tax season.

She can be found reading stories from authors Elissa Malcohn, K.L. Nappier, and Piers Anthony, to name a few. She loves writing down the adventures rattling around in her head as well as poetry that strikes without warning.

She describes her writing style as a blend of her favorite genres. This is her first novel.

Email: author@kishazworld.com.

Website: http://www.kishazworld.com

"Inner Muse" blog: http://innermuse.kishazworld.com

About the Illustrator

J. D. Hollyfield is an artist in many mediums including wood, leather, metal, paint, and graphic design. He currently resides in the mountains of southwestern Virginia.

Visit his website at http://www.jdhollyfield.com

17423203R00134